"How about a kiss, babe?"

Tony sauntered over to Lynn, an insolent smile on his face.

She watched him approach, still unable to believe Tony's transformation. This man was not the serious lawyer she'd always thought of as a buddy. This Tony was all male, all rebel. His white T-shirt molded itself lovingly to his muscled chest, and the fit of his jeans was almost indecent. His hair hung rakishly over his forehead, and even his walk was different.

Lynn tried to back away, but her feet wouldn't move. "Oh, no, you don't. Stop pulling that bad-boy routine on me. It won't work."

A knowing look appeared on his face. "Your body's talking a different language, sugarcakes."

Lord, he was sexy. A coil of excitement tightened within her. "Don't listen," she said.

"Then don't shout," Tony responded, closing the distance between them.

Dear Reader,

Summer brings such pleasant images to mind, ice cream and a day at the beach…great-looking men glistening with suntan lotion…oops! I need to pull my mind back to the topic of Love & Laughter. Nevertheless, in this month's selection, we do have two hunky and adorable heroes to raise your temperatures.

Big, bad boy toy Tony Russo is a lot sexier and much more delicious than Lynn Morgan ever imagined. Lynn convinced her straitlaced lawyer buddy, Tony Russo, to play the role of her no-good boyfriend. More *GQ* than bad-boy material, Lynn feared he couldn't pull it off. But when she saw him transformed into black leather and attitude, she all but forgot about her little scheme. All she could think about was taking a walk on the wild side…in *Operation Gigolo* by Vicki Lewis Thompson.

The last thing pampered rich girl Hannah Nelson wants is a cowboy, but when she's forced to hide out at the Lone Oak Ranch, she begins to see Tyrel Fox in a very different light! The swaggering, sexy cowboy was just so…so elemental, Hannah decided. But would he be more than a change of pace? Find out in *Counterfeit Cowgirl* by Lois Greiman.

Enjoy the summer heat!

Malle Vallik

Malle Vallik
Associate Senior Editor

Vicki Lewis Thompson
OPERATION GIGOLO

HARLEQUIN®

TORONTO • NEW YORK • LONDON
AMSTERDAM • PARIS • SYDNEY • HAMBURG
STOCKHOLM • ATHENS • TOKYO • MILAN • MADRID
PRAGUE • WARSAW • BUDAPEST • AUCKLAND

ISBN 0-373-44047-2

OPERATION GIGOLO

Copyright © 1998 by Vicki Lewis Thompson

A funny thing happened...

The longer I'm married, the more I'm convinced that couples handle big problems just fine. It's the little junk that sends us thumbing through the Yellow Pages under "Lawyers." Take the question of "Who Drives."

As a liberated woman, I felt we should share the job, but my husband is a terrible passenger. He sucks in his breath, winces and mutters as I navigate through traffic. And I'm a good driver. Mostly. "I can't live with a man who hates my driving!" I complained to a friend as I thumbed through the Yellow Pages. "What if I have to drive him around when he gets old. I couldn't stand listening to him sucking in his breath every five minutes." My friend tried hard not to laugh. "Then you could *refuse to drive him*."

Indeed. I put away the Yellow Pages. But come to think of it, there's still the question of "Who Works the Remote Control..."

—Vicki Lewis Thompson

Books by Vicki Lewis Thompson

HARLEQUIN LOVE & LAUGHTER
 5—STUCK WITH YOU
17—ONE MOM TOO MANY
31—GOING OVERBOARD

HARLEQUIN TEMPTATION
624—MR. VALENTINE
642—THE HEARTBREAKER
661—SANTA IN A STETSON
677—MANHUNTING IN MONTANA

To Margaret Falk and Kim Lamb Gregory,
for good times creekside.

And to Sedona Schnebly,
who mercifully contributed her first name instead
of her last to a pioneer settlement beside Oak Creek.

1

"AFTER THIRTY-FIVE YEARS of marriage, your father should let me be on top!"

Lynn Morgan cradled the phone against her shoulder and began sorting through the messages on her desk. "I can't see what difference it makes who's on top, Mom. We're just talking about bodies, here." She glanced up to see Tony Russo looking amused as he leaned against the door-jamb of her office. "Dead bodies," she added for Tony's benefit.

His eyebrows lifted.

"That's beside the point," her mother said. "It's the principle of the thing."

Lynn knew this terrain well. Mediating her parents hare-brained battles had prepared her to become a lawyer, ac-cording to her friends. She offered her mother the expected dose of logic. "Shouldn't it depend on who goes first?"

"That's what *he* says, and it would be just like him to outlive me so he could be on top! I want a guarantee of my final position."

Lynn looked at Tony and rolled her eyes. "Suppose you do go first. You want to be dug up so somebody can slide him in underneath you?"

"Why not?"

"Because we're not talking about rearranging leftovers in the refrigerator! Really, Mom, this is—"

"I can see you don't understand, and I am *not* spending

eternity underneath your father. I want a divorce. You can represent me."

Lynn put down her pile of messages. "Excuse me?"

"A divorce. You are a divorce lawyer, right? Serve your father papers. That should teach him to dictate burial-plot etiquette!"

Lynn leaned forward and focused all her attention on the conversation. "I can't believe you're serious about a divorce."

"Dead serious."

"That's not funny."

"Yes, it is."

To Lynn's amazement, her heart was pounding, as if she were a little kid being threatened with this family disaster instead of a twenty-nine-year-old respected member of the Illinois State Bar. "Listen, buy two plots next to each other in a different part of the cemetery."

"Not on your life! That's my family's plot, and my designated space, and I'm going in it. Let your father find his own plot."

"Look, Mom—" Lynn broke off as a second phone line blinked. "I have another call. Listen to the Muzak a minute and don't go away."

"Don't forget I'm paying long distance, dear."

"I won't forget. Be right back." Lynn put her mother on hold and glanced at Tony.

He pushed away from the doorjamb, his expression sober. He'd always been able to gauge her moods, which made him a valuable friend. "You seem to have your hands full," he said gently. "Why don't I come back later?"

"Please stay. I have a feeling I'm going to need a sounding board when I get through here."

"That's all I need to know." Tony walked over and sat in one of the chairs in front of her desk.

"Thanks. I'll make this as quick as I can." She gave

him a smile as she answered the second line. "Lynn Morgan."

"Your mother's gone bananas," her father said.

"You're telling me. What's all that noise in the background, Dad?" She glanced at Tony, who was shaking his head in sympathy.

"Never mind the noise in the background. I think this is the big one, Peanut. Splitsville. I want you to represent me."

Lynn rested her forehead in her hand. "You, too?"

"What'dya mean, *me, too?* Did she beat me to the punch?"

"No, because I'm not taking either one of you on. Honestly, you sound like two kids fighting over who gets the top bunk."

"It's not just the plot," her father said. "She went to this Seize Your Power seminar, and as if that wasn't enough, she's started taking testosterone, which she claims is because of the Change. But if you ask me, this is one woman who doesn't need testosterone. I tell you, she's developed a real attitude, Peanut."

"She's always had an attitude, Dad." Lynn could see this wasn't going to be a quick-fix situation. "Listen, I'll get back to you on this. Don't do anything rash."

"If you're saying don't move out, I've already got a room at the Naughty and Nice Motel."

"You're kidding." Her father had always joked about staying there, just to get her mother's goat. Surely he hadn't actually done it.

"Well, that part was a mistake."

"You're really at the Naughty and Nice?" She pictured the sleazy motel in a bad part of Springfield, with hookers and drug dealers hanging on every corner.

"I should have checked into the Holiday Inn instead. There's no phones in the room. I'm calling you from the Black Garter Video Shop next door."

Lynn's brain began to spin. "Dad, you can't stay there. That's a rough area."

"I've always wanted to see the place, Peanut. Plus I figured it would send your mother over the moon if I called her from there, but now I can't, because there are no phones."

"Which is another thing. How am I supposed to get in touch with you?"

"I'll figure that out and call you." He lowered his voice again. "You wouldn't believe how some of the women dress around here, Peanut. They—whoops, gotta go. Somebody needs to use the phone, and she looks pretty determined, especially with that earring through her lower lip." He whispered into the phone. *"She's got tattoos everywhere."* Then he hung up.

Lynn took a deep breath before returning to her mother's call. "I have to go, Mom. I'll call you this afternoon, and I certainly hope that by then you and Dad will have come to your senses."

"Talk to the cemetery-plot hog! He's the one who won't listen to reason."

Lynn didn't think it wise to tell her mother the cemetery-plot hog had been on the other line, and that he was currently living in one of the more colorful parts of Springfield. "Goodbye, Mom." She hung up and gazed at Tony. "I can't believe this. They've always squabbled, but it was never serious. It was like living with Ricky and Lucy Ricardo."

"I take it they haven't threatened divorce before."

"Never. But it seems my mother took some motivational seminar and now she's on a rampage fueled by hot flashes. None of that really surprises me, but this talk about divorce…that's just nuts. They've always dreamed of this time, when I'd be on my own and the house would be paid off. Dad took early retirement last year, and…" She stared at Tony as the truth dawned. ''They're bored out of their skulls, aren't they?''

''Looks like. We've sure seen plenty of couples like that come through here.''

''Why did I suppose my parents would be any different?'' Lynn threw her hands in the air. ''Textbook case.''

''Well, I wouldn't go that far. I don't remember any other middle-aged couple filing because they couldn't figure out how to share a cemetery plot.''

''They will *not* file for divorce. Not if I have anything to say about it.'' She crossed her arms and glared at Tony as if he would challenge her claim.

''It'll probably blow over,'' Tony said with a show of conviction.

She wanted to believe him. ''I don't like the sound of things, though. My dad's checked into a motel in the red-light district and my mother's busy shuffling coffins. We're not talking your general run-of-the-mill argument, like whether to give Goliath a bath in the bidet.''

Tony's mouth twitched. ''And Goliath is a...?''

''My father's toy poodle. Mom has a rottweiler named Snookums.'' Lynn glanced at him. ''You're trying not to laugh, aren't you?''

''Not me. Is this funny? I don't see anything funny.''

''Well, at least they've always been entertaining.''

''And you've always had to keep a cool head.''

She leaned back in her chair. ''Yeah, I'm the straitlaced one.''

''Oh, I wouldn't say so. You're the one who suggested we hit a fun park the night after my divorce became final.''

Lynn smiled at the memory. They'd scoured the suburbs until they'd found what she was looking for—bumper cars, pinball machines, noise and people. ''That was a special case. I don't do that for clients, as a rule.''

''Just the *pro bono* ones.''

''Hey, I don't take money from a good friend and colleague. I may need your services sometime. Besides, after the way Michelle—'' She saw the look on his face and wished she hadn't started the sentence in the first place.

"After the way Michelle screwed up my life, you were going to say."

"She was a fool." Lynn couldn't understand Michelle at all, cheating on a man like Tony. His Italian good looks, intelligence and career choice made him what Lynn's mother would call a "catch," but he was also a damned nice guy.

"We both were fools. To be honest, I'd rather talk about your folks' problems than mine."

"Makes sense. Sorry I brought it up." She figured he had to be grieving. The divorce was only six months old, and Michelle had been the center of his universe.

"So, how are you going to keep them from splitting up?" Tony asked.

"Well…" Lynn propped her elbows on the desk and rested her chin on her hands. She and Tony had brainstormed cases many times and she'd come to trust his input. This situation wasn't so different from a complicated point of law. "They're creating conflict because they have no real problems, right?"

"That's my best guess."

"What if I give them one?"

Tony crossed his ankle over his knee and leaned back in the chair. "Like what?"

Lynn thought back to her childhood. "Whenever I used to get in trouble—"

"Yeah, right."

"Okay, it was pretty tame stuff. But considering how my parents debated everything from how to hang toilet paper on the roll to the background pictures on their checks, they never disagreed on how to handle me. On that issue they were a united front."

"Gonna get yourself in trouble?"

She doodled on a pad of paper as her plan took shape.

"Yes, I am. It's time their logical, sane daughter kicked over the traces. And I'm going to get in trouble the old-fashioned way." She looked up. "I'll get pregnant."

Tony lurched forward in the chair. "Hey, not so fast! I don't think this situation requires you to—"

"Not really!" She grinned. "I'll just *say* I'm PG."

"Oh." He sank back in his chair. "I was afraid you were heading to the nearest bar to rustle up a one-night stand."

"For heaven's sake. Does that sound like me? Besides, that would take too long. I need to be pregnant right this minute."

"Lynn, it's a creative idea, but have you thought it through? You're a terrible liar. Even I know that, and you're setting out to fool your parents, the people who raised you."

She tapped her pen against the blotter. "As usual, you've hit on the biggest glitch in my plan. But it's such a good idea."

"You could practice your story."

"I'd have to. Can I practice with you?"

"Sure. I'll even help you come up with it. First of all, you need an identity for the imaginary father of this imaginary kid."

She smiled at him. "I have a feeling you've had some practice with telling tall tales."

"Let's just say I got in more trouble than you did when I was growing up."

"Okay, who's the father? Somebody my parents will go into an apoplectic fit over. Swaggering, macho, cigarette dangling from the corner of his lip, tight jeans, a tattoo. No job prospects, but he's happy I'm working and keeping him in beer. In short, a gigolo."

Tony started to laugh. "You're overdoing it. There's no way they'll buy a story that far-fetched. They'll know you're lying through your teeth the minute you start describing this make-believe lover of yours.''

''Ah, but logical women are notorious for becoming attracted to some sexy loser and having their good sense destroyed by great sex. Besides, I've always been completely honest with them. They'll never expect me to make up an elaborate story like this.'' The thought pricked her conscience. She didn't like the idea of lying to her parents, but she couldn't actually get pregnant to bring them together, so she had no choice.

''Even so, I think they'll want proof for anything this wild.''

''Possibly. But I can't imagine how I could...hmm.'' She gazed at him, narrowing her eyes as she mentally rearranged his appearance. Maybe, just maybe, he was her solution.

Tony shifted in his chair. ''Why are you looking at me like that?''

''Take off your jacket.''

''Why?'' He looked uneasy.

''Humor me.''

He shrugged. ''The lady wants the jacket off, I guess I'll take the jacket off. It's been a strange morning.'' He stood and removed the jacket of his pin-striped suit.

''Now take off the tie.''

He stared at her.

''Come on, Tony. I'm working on a concept here.''

He sighed and took off the tie.

''Now unbutton the first three or four buttons of your shirt, and mess up your hair.''

''Mess up my—'' He looked at her as if she'd gone totally bonkers.

She got up and came around the desk. ''Like this.'' She rubbed her fingers vigorously over his scalp.

''Hey!'' He leaped back. ''Who are you and what have you done with Lynn?''

"That's not quite the look I had in mind." She started toward him.

He backed up a step. "Stay away from me, woman."

"Oh, relax. And hold still. This will just take a minute." Grasping his shoulder to keep him near her, she reached up and combed her fingers through his hair so it fell over his forehead, giving him a look of careless nonchalance instead of his usual combed-back, businesslike style. She was pleasantly surprised by the silky feel of his hair and the solid muscles under his dress shirt. She prolonged the task a little.

He smelled good, she noticed, catching a whiff of an after-shave that she'd always associated with him but never allowed herself to consider sexy. "Now for the buttons," she said, undoing the first four.

"Lynn, is this a seduction?" Tony asked.

"Nope."

"Didn't think so. You're beginning to worry me."

"I just want to check something out." She stepped back, hands on hips, to survey her work.

The transformation was remarkable. Gone was the up-and-coming young lawyer who spent his days immersed in legal briefs and courtroom procedure, the man who always arrived at the office early and left late, a bundle of files under his arm. This Tony was hot. He looked as if he had one thing on his mind, and it certainly didn't involve paperwork. A tremor of sexual desire shook her poise. Michelle must have gone to stupid school.

But the main thing was that Tony would be perfect for her scheme. She looked up at him and smiled. "Tony, how about if you—"

"Don't even go there." He shook his head and backed away. "I was afraid that was where you were headed. I failed drama class in high school. Performances aren't my long suit." He started refastening the buttons on his shirt.

"Are you joking? You're a lawyer!"

He smiled at that. "Yeah, but we're talking about something a lot more complicated."

"No, we're not. You put on a show every time you step into that courtroom. This would just be a different kind. I said I might need your services. Turns out I do."

"I meant legal services." He reached for the tie he'd thrown over the back of the chair.

"I don't need legal services. I need a sexy-looking guy for Operation Gigolo. To my surprise, you'd do very nicely."

He stopped in the act of knotting his tie and gazed at her. "To your *surprise?* That's not very flattering."

She blushed. "Well, I just never thought of you in that way, because you're always so...so polished-looking." *So married.*

"Polished-looking. As in slick?" He finished with the tie and picked up his jacket.

"No. You look perfectly wonderful, like an ad from *GQ*."

"Some women go for that type."

"Of course they do!"

"But you don't?" He put on his jacket and adjusted the lapels.

"I didn't say that." Damn, this was a bog she hadn't intended to get into. Six months after a divorce was a prime time for a rebound attraction, and she didn't want to be the target for that sort of temporary affair. "I just—we're way off the subject here. Tony, please help me out. It won't take much of your time to meet my parents. Once they see you, they'll start a campaign to break us up, which will bring them together again. They can succeed in breaking us up, and then I'll conveniently miscarry the love child, and life will return to normal. I happen to know you haven't taken much time off lately."

"And to remedy that, you're offering me a fun-filled trip to Springfield, where I get to act like a jerk and hopefully get pitched out of your parents' house on my butt? Gee, you sure know how to tempt a guy.''

''Actually, I wasn't thinking of Springfield. Ever been to Sedona, Arizona?''

''Nope. Just seen pictures of all those red rocks. Pretty impressive.''

''It is. And my parents honeymooned there. The summer rush would be over now, so I probably could get reservations at the same cottages on the banks of Oak Creek where they stayed thirty-five years ago. I'm sure I can convince them that they have to come,'' she said, patting her stomach.

He looked more interested at the prospect of going to Sedona. ''What if your folks demand separate sleeping accommodations?''

''I'll tell them they have to share because there were only two available when I called.'' She folded her arms and repressed a smile of triumph. As a lawyer she'd learned to read expressions, and she could see that Tony was beginning to consider her idea. ''What do you say? An all-expense-paid long weekend in a beautiful spot in exchange for wearing tight jeans and flexing your muscles.''

He hesitated. ''Is your dad a violent man?''

''Absolutely not. He might try to talk you to death, but he wouldn't challenge you to a fistfight or anything, if that's what you mean. I promise this is low risk.''

''You don't have somebody else who could do this? I thought you were dating a guy named Edgar.''

She grimaced. ''I was, but in the first place my parents have met him, and in the second place, I broke it off a couple of months ago, and in the third place, Edgar could never play a convincing stud-muffin.''

''Is that right?'' He looked pleased with the information.

''That's right.'' Tony was awfully cute, she thought, cuter than she'd allowed herself to realize.

"I don't know." He glanced at her. "It'll take a lot to rub the polish off, don't you think?"

Thinking about turning him into a modern-day James Dean sent delicious shivers through her. Transforming Tony. What a fun concept. "No, I don't think it'll take all that much," she said. "Although it would be helpful if you had a tattoo."

"It would, huh?"

"Yeah, but I wouldn't expect that kind of sacrifice. Maybe we could try one of those temporary kinds." She waited, hoping he was as intrigued by the whole charade concept as she was.

"Okay, I'll do it."

She smiled. "Thanks, Tony. You're a real friend. I'll let you know when I've made the arrangements. Is there any weekend I should avoid?"

"Not really. My social calendar isn't what you'd call jammed."

So he wasn't dating anyone yet, she thought. He really was ripe for a rebound affair. She'd have to be careful. "It takes time after a divorce."

"Yeah. But hey, things are looking up. I've just been invited to spend a long weekend with a beautiful woman."

She laughed, as if he'd made a joke, but it didn't feel like a joke. "Thanks for the compliment." She liked having him call her beautiful, but she couldn't encourage him to think there could be something between them. "But I'm afraid it'll be a platonic weekend."

He shrugged. "It's a start." As he walked out the door, he paused and turned back to her. "Oh, and about that tattoo…"

"Don't worry about it. I'll check into the temporary kind. It may not be all that important, anyway."

"You don't have to check into anything." He gave her a killer smile. "I already have one."

2

THE NIGHT BEFORE the trip to Sedona, Tony dug in his closet, unearthing memories as he worked, and came up with a couple of pairs of jeans he'd worn in high school. Michelle had begged him to get rid of this old stuff, claiming that he had no reason to keep it.

But there was a reason. He didn't want to totally lose the connection to the hell-raiser he'd been back then, and the clothes helped make that connection. He smiled to himself. Lynn had no idea that the punk she'd described as her parents' worst nightmare was Tony Russo fourteen years ago.

The tattoo was a souvenir from his senior year, his way of balancing the embarrassment of ending up the valedictorian. When he got drunk with his buddies one night and was caught spray-painting Class of '84 on the hood of the principal's Caddy, the school board hadn't wanted to let him graduate, let alone give the valedictory speech. His mother had pleaded his case and suggested his penance be cleaning gum off the bottom of the bleachers. To this day the smell of chewing gum made him sick to his stomach.

He pulled open a dresser drawer and dug in the back for the white T-shirts he hardly ever wore these days. They'd seen a lot of use at one time, and they felt soft and familiar in his grip. He kept one out for the plane ride and tossed the rest in a large duffel bag just as the phone on the bedside table rang. As he picked up the receiver, he wondered if Lynn had some last-minute instructions for him.

"Tony?"

Michelle. And she sounded as if she'd been crying, dammit. He tried to harden his heart. "Yeah, Michelle."

"Are you busy?"

He tensed. "Kind of. What's wrong?"

"I'd like…" She sniffed. "I'd like to come over, if it's okay."

He glanced at the clock. Michelle in tears, wanting to see him at eleven at night, couldn't mean anything but trouble with Jerry. Jerry, his stockbroker and health-club buddy, the guy who'd spent his evenings playing handball with Tony and his afternoons playing bedroom games with Michelle.

"I know it's late." Michelle's voice quavered. "I just…need to talk to somebody."

He sighed. "Okay."

"Thanks, Tony."

"Don't mention it. That's what ex-husbands are for." As he hung up, he wondered why he hadn't told her to get lost. She deserved to be told that, after the way she'd treated him. He was a sucker when it came to the women in his life, just as his brothers and sisters had always said. They'd advised him to use the adultery issue to make sure Michelle didn't get a dime, but instead he'd agreed to split their assets down the middle. His family called that stupid, but he'd handled enough divorce cases to know that nobody was blameless. He'd been concentrating too hard on his job, leaving her alone too much and paving the way for Jerry to step in.

For the first couple of years of marriage everything had been wonderful. She'd been his Uptown Girl, just like in the Billy Joel song that had been such a hit back in high school. It hadn't hurt that she'd looked a little like Christie Brinkley, and he'd always identified with a working-class type like Billy Joel. Then he'd become more involved in his law career and had never quite noticed that the magic was slipping away.

He repressed thoughts of Michelle and his mistakes as best he could and continued packing. As much as he'd resisted the idea of Operation Gigolo when Lynn had first proposed it, he'd finally realized he'd be a fool to refuse. He'd wanted to ask her out for weeks, but he'd held back, afraid she'd think a recently divorced guy was a bad risk. As family-law specialists they'd both seen how divorce screwed up anyone's judgment concerning the opposite sex.

He figured she'd think any interest on his part was strictly on the rebound from Michelle. At this point, Tony wondered if she might not be right. Maybe it was a good thing Michelle was coming over. He hadn't seen her for six months.

He stared at his open duffel and wondered if he'd forgotten anything. Cigarettes. Lynn had said something about a cigarette dangling from the corner of his mouth, but he'd given up smoking years ago. Then he remembered that Sam, another lawyer friend, had left half a pack behind over the weekend when he'd dropped over to watch a Cubs game on TV. Tony walked into the kitchen and rummaged through his catchall drawer until he found the cigarettes he'd tossed in there, meaning to return them.

Shaking one out, he found matches in the same drawer and cupped the flame as he lit up. Funny how the action, after so many years, brought back the old swagger. It brought back a slight cough, too. He'd never been a heavy smoker, doing it more for effect than for the nicotine buzz. That had made quitting more bearable than it had been for some of his high-school pals. If he limited himself to one cigarette whenever he was around Lynn's parents, he shouldn't get hooked again.

The doorbell rang, and he took another drag on the cigarette before walking over to let Michelle in.

"Tony!" Sobbing, she flung herself dramatically into his arms.

He damn near burned her with the cigarette as he caught her. "Easy, Michelle." Holding the cigarette a safe distance away, he put an arm around her trembling shoulders and guided her to the couch. "What's the problem?"

She plopped down and gazed at him through brimming eyes. The glue on her right eyelash was failing, and the black fringe dangled from her eyelid, dancing like a drunk butterfly each time she blinked.

"Eyelash alert," he said automatically. He'd forgotten how lousy she'd always been at putting them on, but she persisted, believing that her own blond lashes were too short and undramatic. Her hair wasn't as thick as she'd like it to be, either, and he knew that at this very moment she had fake hair fastened in with her own. He'd never been able to run his fingers through Michelle's hair without danger of permanent injury from the metal clips.

"Thanks." She reached up and pulled the eyelash off, which left her with an interesting effect—one eye ready to party and the other one ready for sleep. She began to sniffle again and searched through her minuscule shoulder bag. "Damn, you can't put anything in these. Do you have a—"

"Here." He pulled a handkerchief from his back pocket and handed it to her. As she blew her nose, he took another drag on the cigarette and stubbed it out in the ashtray.

"Oh, Tony..." She wiped her eyes and took a shaky breath. "I should never have left you for Jerry."

His heart clutched. That had been what he'd wanted to hear for months, right? So why wasn't he feeling a thrill of triumph, instead of this uneasy dread? "What's happened?" he asked.

"He sucks his teeth."

Tony laughed. It wasn't a kind thing to do, and he controlled it as quickly as he could. "You didn't notice that before?"

"Well, sort of, but I didn't think I'd care. Did you...did you ever notice that about him?"

"Yeah, but when you're playing handball it's not a big item of concern."

"That's not all. He wears some of his underwear until it's dangling from the elastic by about three threads." She glanced at Tony. "You knew that, too, didn't you?"

He shrugged. "We dressed in the same locker room. Sure I noticed." After the fact, he wished he'd checked out Jerry's studly endowments, too. The guy had stolen his wife, and Tony couldn't help wondering if Jerry was more than a good listener.

"I threw all the raggedy ones away today, and he yelled at me. Then I yelled at him about his teeth, and he yelled about stabbing himself on my hair clips, and then he said my eyelashes gave him a rash and looked stupid."

"Then he shouldn't wear your eyelashes, should he?"

She giggled. "You know what I mean. Do my eyelashes look stupid, Tony?"

"Uh, not when they're both attached." Which was seldom, he remembered. But he'd loved her, idiosyncrasies and all.

She sighed. "You were so easy to live with."

But she hadn't been, he was remembering now. With each year, she'd needed more reassurance that she was beautiful and desirable. He'd grown tired of the constant questioning, and his answers must have become tired and clichéd, too. That could have had a lot to do with the Jerry episode. Nothing like an affair to shore up somebody's ego.

"I thought you were in love with Jerry," he said quietly. He'd expected to feel pain when he said that, but miraculously, he didn't.

"I thought I was too, but how can you love somebody who sucks his teeth and wears Swiss-cheese underwear?"

For the first time in the whole mess he was beginning to understand. He'd committed himself to love and cherish, in sickness and in health, through hairpieces and dangling eyelashes, but Michelle had been operating on a much shallower level. And she still was.

She took a deep breath. "I thought about all this during the cab ride over here. I think you and I should give it another try."

"You spent the whole cab ride thinking about that?" He heard the sarcasm in his voice and decided that wouldn't help matters. "I'm sorry. That was uncalled for."

"What was uncalled for?"

He gazed at her. She hadn't caught the sarcasm. For her, a cab ride across Chicago was plenty of time to consider changing her life, and the lives of those around her. Like so many others who came through his law office, he'd invested his love in the wrong person. But it didn't seem to be invested there anymore. Still, they'd shared a lot, and he wanted her to be as happy as she could be, considering the emotional handicaps she had to overcome.

"I don't think getting back together is the answer," he said gently.

"But I do, Tony."

"Well, I don't, and I'll tell you why. One of the reasons you didn't notice irritating little things about me was that I wasn't here much. When I was, I was on my best behavior. Eventually, though, you'd find out that I whistle off-key and I'm a manic channel surfer."

"Your whistling's cute."

"You haven't heard much of it. I've been at the office, trying to forge this career. Ask Sam about my whistling."

"Whistling wouldn't bother me. And you hardly ever watch TV."

"Ah, but one day I'll have more time, and then I'd use that remote to drive you crazy."

"Tony, none of that matters. What matters is—"

"What, Michelle? What matters?"

"That we love each other." Her blue eyes grew dreamy.

He felt a nostalgic tug, remembering how he used to respond to that look of hers. "Ten months ago you told me you loved Jerry."

"I was so wrong."

"Then learn to love him."

The dreamy look dissolved as she stared at him. "What?"

"I'm sure Jerry has lots of good qualities."

"Name one."

"Hey." He chuckled. "Don't ask me to do that. I'm willing to be charitable, but listing Jerry's good qualities is a little much, even for a sap like me."

"See, you don't like him!"

"No, but you need to. You left our marriage for him, and you need to find things about him that you can cherish, things that make the holey underwear and the teeth-sucking seem like small change."

"I thought you'd understand." She flounced to her feet, looking petulant. "But you're just making fun of me."

He stood and shoved his hands in his pockets. "Actually, I've never been more serious in my life."

"I don't believe that. I think—" Her eyes narrowed. "You've found someone, haven't you?"

"No." A picture of Lynn flashed through his mind. He'd bet he could run his fingers through her rich brown hair without being stabbed. But as of now Lynn was only a good friend and their current arrangement was just a charade to fool her parents. "No, there's no one," he said.

"Then why won't you consider getting back together?"

He searched for the words that would make her understand without hurting her. "Look, I still care about you. I probably always will. But that deep, down-to-the-bone commitment I used to have, that feeling that I'd give my life for you—that's gone, Michelle. I didn't know that until you came over tonight, but I know it now."

"We could get it back!"

He shook his head. "I don't think so. Make up with Jerry. Work on what you have." He smiled. "Buy him some sexy new underwear."

"You *are* making fun of me." She glared at him.

"Honest, I'm not."

"You really don't think we should start over?"

He shook his head.

"Then I might as well go home to Jerry."

He followed her to the door and opened it. "That's what I'm saying. He's your best shot, not me."

She started into the hall, then paused and glanced back at him. "Are you sure my eyelashes don't look stupid?"

"They're part of you, Michelle. Don't change a thing." She smiled. "Thanks." Then she frowned, as if trying to remember something. "Were you smoking when I first came in?"

It was just like her to be so wrapped up in herself that she hadn't noticed until now. He thought about explaining and decided not to. "Yeah, I was."

She shuddered. "Yuck. I would hate that."

"See? We're really not right for each other anymore." Then, to get a laugh out of her, he sucked loudly on his teeth.

It worked. She laughed. "We had some good times, didn't we, Tony?"

A whisper of what he used to feel for her passed over his heart and was gone. "Yes, we did. Take care of yourself, Michelle."

"You, too."

He watched her walk down the hallway and could find no regret remaining in his soul. It was a good way to begin tomorrow's adventure.

LYNN LIVED at the opposite end of Chicago from Tony, so they hadn't seen much percentage in sharing a cab to O'Hare. She'd agreed to meet him at the gate, and as she stood in the waiting area, fidgeting with the handle of her rolling carry-on, she took several calming breaths. Preperformance jitters, probably, similar to the ones she got before stepping into the courtroom.

Except this nervousness had a special edge to it. She'd come up with the idea in the heat of the crisis, and she still loved the plan, but she'd had time to consider the ramifications in the days since then. For example, she'd have to put on a convincing display of affection for Tony, which meant putting their arms around each other a lot, not to mention kissing and nuzzling in public whenever possible. The more sickening the display, the better. The only physical contact she'd had with Tony was limited to handshakes and the one time she'd hugged him after the divorce decree was handed down. Yet she couldn't imagine how they'd practice such a thing, so they'd have to hope they looked natural doing something they'd never done with each other before.

And then there was the matter of sharing a cottage with one king-size bed in it. She hadn't figured out how they'd handle the sleeping arrangements, and she'd been too chicken to bring up the subject when she'd discussed the plans with Tony. Maybe there was a couch. Or they could put a rolled blanket down the center of the bed, the way her mother used to divide up the space when her cousin Sherilee had come to spend the night. But Tony wasn't exactly Sherilee.

No, he certainly wasn't. She spotted him strolling down the terminal, an insolent smile on his face. His white T-shirt molded itself lovingly to his muscled chest, and the fit of his jeans was almost indecent. His hair hung rakishly over his forehead, and even his walk was different. Lynn swallowed. Dear Lord, what had she let herself in for? He wasn't even Tony anymore.

When he reached her, he dropped his duffel bag to the

floor and swept her into his arms. "Hey, baby," he said in a low voice. Then he kissed her, hard.

Nearby, somebody whistled in admiration.

At first, Lynn was too shocked to react, and too fascinated by the feel of Tony's lips on hers. Finally, she gained enough command of herself to try shoving him away. He didn't shove very easily.

"Where are you going, sweet thing?" he asked, holding her fast as he gave her a lazy smile. "Aren't you glad to see your lover boy?"

Her heart hammered as she saw the light of desire in his dark eyes. She had to remind herself he was playing a role. "Tony, let go of me. You're carrying this a bit far. We don't have to start our act just yet."

He rubbed her back, and his hand crept lower, to cup her behind. "Don't you think we need to warm up to it, baby doll?"

Damned if he wasn't turning her on with this macho-stud routine. Aware of several people staring, she spoke through clenched teeth. "Not in the middle of the airport, we don't."

He gave her a wink and a gentle pinch on the bottom. "If you say so, sweetcakes."

She stepped away from him, her cheeks hot. "Honestly, Tony."

He grinned at her, looking a little more like his normal self. "I thought before we climbed on this bird you might appreciate a sneak preview, in case you wanted to back out of the deal."

She adjusted her clothes. "Um, I…no, I don't want to back out. I just wasn't expecting…" Damn, she was stammering like a high-school kid with a crush. Unable to take her gaze from him, she grasped for something sensible to talk about. "Where did you get those clothes? They don't look new."

"From the back of my closet."

"You used to wear stuff like that?"

"Sure. All the time." He tucked the pack of cigarettes more securely in the roll of his T-shirt sleeve. Beneath it, his biceps flexed, drawing attention to the dragon tattooed there.

She stared at that rippling dragon. That's right, he'd said he had a tattoo, and there it was, real as could be. Forcing her gaze back to his face, she cleared her throat. "Tony, are you telling me that you used to be—"

"The guy your mother warned you about. Yup. Drove too fast, drank too much, tried my best to reduce the population of vir—"

"Spare me the details of your conquests."

"Not conquests," he said softly. "I wasn't a predator, Lynn. I never took what wasn't offered."

No doubt the offers were plentiful, she thought. At seventeen she wouldn't have dared hook up with a guy like this...yet how she'd wanted to. Her teenage sexual fantasies had been filled with tight jeans, motorcycles and muscle. And now she had to wonder if this escapade had been partly born of those unsatisfied fantasies. If so, she could be in a lot of trouble, because Tony had turned out to be the real thing.

She took a deep breath. "I had no idea you had that kind of background. I assumed, with your degree from Harvard, that you'd been a..."

"Nerd?" He laughed. "I've worked hard turning myself into a nerd in the past fourteen years, so maybe I've succeeded. Hey, I think they just called our flight."

"They did?" She hadn't heard a thing. Apparently, one of the jets could have plowed nose first into the terminal and she wouldn't have noticed that, either. She needed to snap out of it, and fast. "Then I guess we'd better go."

He gestured toward the jetway. "I'll follow you." His gaze became hooded and suggestive. "I sure do enjoy walking behind a chick with a tight...schedule."

"Tony Russo!"

He winked at her. "Get used to it, Lynn. You're supposed to be loving comments like that, remember? Looks like I'll have to coach the witness on the plane ride." He gave her a shallow bow. "After you."

3

When they reached their seats, Lynn started to put her suitcase in the overhead bin, as she always did.

"Not while I'm around, sugarcakes." Tony took hold of the suitcase.

"I can do it." She hated helpless females, and she continued with the task.

"Don't make me get rough, woman." Still holding on to the suitcase, Tony loomed over her. Incoming passengers pressed from behind, plastering them together. "Women's lib detoured right around this boy."

Her body reacted to the close quarters by becoming aroused. Great. "What are you talking about? You're very liberated!"

He leaned down and murmured in her ear. "For the next four days, I'm a chauvinist pig, remember? Now give me that suitcase and go sit down."

"And which seat did you want me to take, darling?" she asked with exaggerated humility.

He smiled. "Much better, except for the teensy bit of sarcasm. You can have the window."

She batted her eyelashes. "But that would put you in the middle seat, and I can't believe you'd be happy there, sweetheart."

"That depends. Maybe somebody as hot as you will take the aisle seat, and I can be the filling in a babe sandwich."

Lynn groaned and edged into the far seat as Tony hoisted

her suitcase into the overhead bin with an admirable display of biceps and triceps. He heaved his duffel in after it.

She noticed the gaze of many female passengers avidly following Tony's moves. Their attention would return briefly to Lynn, then swing back to Tony, and the speculation was obvious in their expressions. She'd worn her normal traveling outfit—silk blouse, tailored shorts and jacket, nylons and designer shoes. The contrast with Tony's more casual clothes made him seem younger, somehow. In fact, he looked exactly like what she'd intended for her parents to see—her boy toy.

When he sat down beside her, she leaned toward him and lowered her voice. "Thanks, but I really think you're laying it on a little thick."

"According to you, that's not possible. You want your parents frothing at the mouth, right?"

"Well...yes, but—"

"And from your reaction to my act, you need a lot of practice being my main squeeze."

She gazed at him and shook her head in wonder. "I can't believe I'm sitting next to Anthony J. Russo, attorney-at-law."

"You're not. You're sitting next to Tony The Tomcat." His dark eyes twinkled. "Around Midvale High, they used to say I was born to prowl."

"Oh, please." She struggled to hang on to a more comfortable reality. "You know, I could really screw up your image around the office with that information."

"I know. I'm trusting you not to."

"Of course I won't. But honestly, Tony, this is an incredible transformation."

He smiled. "Oh, you ain't seen nothin' yet, sweetface."

"My God, I've created a monster."

"The better to freak out your old man and old lady, hot pants."

Lynn rolled her eyes. "We may not even get to Sedona.

At this rate we'll accomplish the mission thirty seconds from the time we meet them at the Phoenix airport.'' She glanced beyond him as a young man in a ponytail consulted his ticket and sat down next to Tony. "Too bad, lover boy. No babe sandwich," she murmured.

"Well, damn." He leaned over and gave her a quick kiss on the lips. "Guess I'll have to make do with you."

"Tony!" Her cheeks burning, she pulled back, but she was limited in how much distance she could put between them. She pretended that she didn't like his outrageous advances, but the problem was she liked them too much. Her lips tingled and she wished he'd kiss her again...and stay a while next time.

He shook his head and clucked his tongue at her. "You've got to quit shying away or your parents will never believe this stunt. I suggest we draw up ground rules and a plan of action."

"A plan. That's a good idea." She couldn't possibly talk about it now without hyperventilating. She grabbed the airline magazine out of the seat pocket in front of her. "Maybe during lunch." She started rapidly flipping the pages.

"I'll be damned. Lynn Morgan, attorney-at-law, is flustered."

She glanced up at him. "No, I'm not."

"Yes, you are." He gazed at her, a smile on his face. "Ever since I appeared in the terminal you've been a basket case. I never thought I'd see the day that you'd totally lose your cool, Counselor."

"This is an unusual situation." She looked at the magazine, desperate for a way out of the conversation. "Oh, look. An article about forcing tulip bulbs. I've always wondered how they do that." She pretended great interest in the first few paragraphs.

"From what I hear, if you know how to stroke a tulip, no force is necessary."

Zip, a surge of desire dived straight down to the tender spot where it would do the most damage. "You're incorrigible," she muttered, trying to sound nonchalant and failing miserably.

"That's the idea." He leaned back in his chair. "Okay, I'll leave you alone to read about the mating habits of flowers."

As if she could concentrate on anything but keeping her breathing steady. She abandoned the armrest between them because using it meant he might rest his arm there, too, and she wasn't up to that much contact at the moment. Still, there was no avoiding this potent male by her side whose knee brushed against hers occasionally and whose shoulder touched her shoulder whenever he shifted in his seat. And there was no turning back. The plane roared to the end of the runway and lifted into the sky.

Tony was surprised and secretly delighted that his behavior had Lynn so shook up. In her logical way, she might have thought they could pretend to be lovers to fool her parents and keep their emotions strictly out of it. He'd acted on impulse, kissing her like that when he met her at the terminal, but boy, had he enjoyed it. And he'd be allowed—required, in fact—to kiss her a lot more. If this morning was any indication of how she'd react, this should be a very interesting trip.

Glancing at the magazine in her hand, he concluded that either she was a very slow reader, which wasn't likely, or she was staring at the page without seeing it. She was probably contemplating what she'd let herself in for with her clever little scheme.

He decided to let her muse on that for a while and struck up a conversation with the man seated next to him. The guy was a psychologist named Jeff, and he became increasingly friendly as Tony revealed himself to be more educated than his manner of dress would have suggested. They exchanged cards with promises that Tony would contact Jeff if he ever needed counseling and Jeff would contact Tony if he ever needed legal advice.

"Which I very well might, one of these days," Jeff said as lunch arrived.

"Give me a call," Tony said. "Now, if you'll excuse me, I have a strategy session scheduled with my...traveling companion."

"Sure." Jeff looked openly curious, but he didn't ask any questions.

Tony unwrapped his silverware and glanced at Lynn. "We need to talk. We'll be in Phoenix before you know it."

She concentrated very hard on sprinkling pepper on her salad. "Okay, I'll admit it. I'm nervous."

"We could land in Phoenix, tell them we had a terrible argument on the plane and catch the next flight home."

She put down the pepper package and looked at him. "No, we can't. I know the strategy will work, and it's all set up, but I—" She glanced away and took a deep breath. "I'm afraid your original assessment might be right. I'm not used to lying, and I may be too...too inhibited to pull this off."

His heart went out to her. She wanted so much to help her parents, but it went against her natural truthfulness and modesty. He liked those traits in her, but they would ruin her plan unless she overrode them for a few days.

He searched for a way to put her more at ease. "Maybe if you direct things, instead of me just foisting myself on you, it won't seem so invasive. We could have signals, like in baseball."

A tiny smile appeared on her sweet mouth. "Signals?"

"Yeah, like clearing your throat means I stick my tongue in your ear, scratching your nose means a French kiss, and brushing your shoulder means I grab your—"

"Forget it," she said quickly, the color rising in her cheeks.

"The signals? Or grabbing?"

"Both."

"We can think of a better idea than the signals, but if we're going to put on a completely nauseating show, I should probably do a little grabbing. In fact, you should, too. Parents hate that, but it will be very convincing. I'll grab easy, I promise."

"Where...where would you...?"

"The standard places."

"I don't have any *standard places*."

He laughed and gulped some water, suddenly needing a drink. "Sorry. I absolutely agree. Your places are way above average."

She gazed at him for a long moment, her expression revealing her turmoil.

"It was a joke," he said.

"I know." She sighed and leaned back against the seat. "Maybe this is hopeless. I'm probably not up to it."

"Hey, that doesn't sound like the Lynn Morgan I know." He studied her tense profile. There was character in that face, and although she wasn't a blond bombshell like Michelle, she had an elegant beauty that appealed to him. Appealed to him a lot. "The Lynn Morgan I work with every day doesn't give up before she's even started."

She turned her head to look at him. "It's a tougher job than I imagined, Tony. How in the world am I going to manage?"

"By relaxing, and thinking of it as play instead of serious stuff." He smiled. "If we're going to make fools of ourselves this weekend, we might as well enjoy it. Loosen up and have fun with this crazy scheme of yours."

She held his gaze, and gradually the tense lines around her eyes and mouth eased, and mischief began to dance in her brown eyes. "Okay. Just what do you have in mind, big boy?"

Whoa. He hadn't expected her to pack such a wallop.

He wasn't going to have to fake this attraction. "Just keep looking at me like that, and we'll have it made," he said.

"I thought you wanted to plan our moves."

He swallowed. He'd like to make one on her right here, right now. Planning ahead might be overkill. "I think when the time comes, we'll know what to do."

"You're sure?"

Oh, yes. "Just keep in mind that we're supposed to be so filled with love and lust that we can't keep our hands off each other." He took another drink of water. Surely his hand wasn't trembling. Nothing bothered Tony The Tomcat.

"Excuse me," Jeff said, putting his hand on Tony's arm. "But I couldn't help overhearing some of your conversation. I have some knowledge in this area, and I think you're both making a big mistake."

Tony glanced at him in amazement. "Look, Jeff, with all due respect, I don't think we need your—"

"You should see the color of your aura right now. And hers. You're both troubled." Jeff smiled. "Let me help. No charge."

Lynn leaned forward and gave him a puzzled glance. "I must be missing something."

Jeff faced her, his expression earnest. "Take pride in who you are! If society makes you ashamed, just surround yourself with white light, stand up and say, 'This is me. I may be different from you, but that doesn't make me less valuable, or less moral.'"

Tony had thought the guy was fairly rational, but he was reassessing that conclusion. "Listen, Jeff, are you overdue for some medication, or something? I'll be glad to call the flight attendant and get you a—"

"I'm having a little trouble with my sun center these

days, but meditation and color therapy seems to be taking care of it. In fact, I should be wearing my chakra glasses right this minute. Thanks for reminding me." He reached into his shirt pocket and pulled out a pair of canary-tinted wraparound sunglasses and put them on.

Tony stared at him.

"That's better," Jeff said, as if it was perfectly normal to wear yellow sunglasses inside an airplane. He patted Tony's knee. "My practice is filled with people of your persuasion, my friend. I advise you both to confess the truth to your parents. I promise you'll be cleansed by the experience, and so will they. After all, everybody's coming out these days."

"What?" Tony instinctively rose out of his seat and bumped into the lap tray, upsetting his water glass into his lunch. Beside him, he could hear Lynn's muffled laughter. "Look, Jeff, I'm not—"

"Oh, Tony, of course you are. Why else would a lawyer feel it necessary to dress like that? You're trying to project some macho image to throw people off the track, but it's not working, and you know it."

"I am *not gay.*" Tony realized he'd said that a little loud, and people were turning in their seats to check out the conversation.

Lynn cleared her throat and leaned over Tony's destroyed lunch to gaze at Jeff. "He's really not," she said. Her lips were twitching, as if she was having a hell of a time keeping a straight face. "Dressing that way was my idea."

"I'm not surprised." Jeff looked knowing. "You're projecting your own desire to act that role onto Tony. Be courageous! Wear the tight jeans and T-shirt yourself! Go for the motorcycle boots and the tattoo! Believe me, you'll feel so much better."

"Okay, here's the deal," Lynn said. "My parents are having some problems, and so—"

''There you go. I'll bet they're struggling with sexual issues, themselves. Clear the air for all of you, and you might have more in common than you think.''

Tony spoke through clenched teeth. ''We...are... straight. All of us. Straight as a board.''

Jeff smiled and settled back against his seat. ''You are so typical of my other clients. So defensive. You have my card. When you're ready to honor that side of yourself, give me a call. I know a great sweat lodge.'' He put on a pair of earphones and switched on a small tape recorder he had in his shirt pocket.

Tony had stuck Jeff's business card in his wallet, and now it seemed to burn a hole in his butt. He longed to get it out and tear it into little pieces, but that would give Jeff more evidence that he was being defensive.

So he turned to look at Lynn instead. Yes, he was definitely heterosexual. He wanted to wring her neck for helping him get into such a ridiculous conversation, but even more he wanted to plant kisses on that neck.

She pressed her lips together and her eyes brimmed with laughter.

He lowered his voice. ''You enjoyed that, didn't you?''

She nodded.

''There goes my bid for the presidential nomination.''

''Tony! I didn't know you had that kind of ambition.''

''I don't, but if I did, I'd be dead in the water, and it's all your fault.''

Her eyes rounded in innocence. ''My fault? I defended you.''

''You were trying not to laugh the whole time. Very unconvincing defense, Counselor.''

''Want me to try again?''

''God, no. The harder we protest, the more he believes.'' He found his own sense of humor gradually returning. ''I've been accused of many things in my life, but never that.''

"You're a very good friend, Tony. I'm sorry I laughed when you were dealing with him, but you have to admit it's kind of funny. I never imagined somebody would draw that conclusion from our discussion."

"No telling what the rest of the plane thinks, either, after I shouted out my sexual preference."

"It doesn't matter. I know you're all male." She paused and gave him a questioning look. "Aren't you?"

"You'll pay for that one, Morgan," he said with a grim smile. And as the plane started its descent into the Phoenix area, he started anticipating the ways he might prove to her that he was, indeed, all male.

WHEN LYNN MADE everyone's plane reservations, she'd co-ordinated the flights so that her parents would be waiting at the gate when she and Tony arrived. She had a grand entrance in mind.

After the plane landed and people began leaving their seats, Tony leaned toward her. "Let's give our boy Jeff a head start," he said in an undertone.

Just then Jeff stood and laid a hand on Tony's shoulder. Lynn smothered a smile as Tony flinched.

Jeff leaned over, and the crystal on a cord around his neck dangled next to Tony's ear. "Keep me posted," Jeff said. "I'm there for you if you need a friend."

"Right." Tony didn't look at him.

"See you later." Jeff gave Tony's shoulder a squeeze and moved into the aisle.

"Not if I see you first," Tony muttered under his breath.

"Don't worry," Lynn said, taking pity on him. "Have you ever once met someone again after sitting next to them on a plane?"

"I guess you're right. Is he gone?"

"He just walked out the door. I think we're safe."

"Then let's go play heterosexual games for your parents' benefit."

Lynn's heart pounded as she pulled her wheeled carry-on down the jetway with Tony close behind. As long as she focused on her parents' threat of divorce, she'd be fine. To avoid that, she'd be willing to do almost anything. She knew they loved each other, and they'd be miserable if they separated. She'd be miserable, too. They'd been a trusted anchor all her life, and she wouldn't give up that feeling of safety without a fight.

Just before she emerged from the jetway, she paused and turned to Tony. "Ready?"

"Yup. As soon as we're clear of the tunnel, I'm putting my arm around you. Look adoring."

"Adoring. Got it." She stepped out of the jetway.

The next few seconds delivered one sensory shock after another. First, she glimpsed her mother, whose usual conservative hairstyle had been replaced by the electrocuted look. The wild red curls were at complete odds with the stern expression on Gladys Morgan's face, but they perfectly matched the lime green, shimmery material of her tank top and shorts. Lynn almost expected to see in-line skates on her mother's feet, but instead she wore platform shoes.

About that time, Tony pulled her close and nuzzled her neck. "Kiss me, gorgeous," he murmured.

"Tony, my mother—"

"Your mother needs to see some liplock."

"She's…oh my God." Lynn's gaze slid a few feet across the terminal and she discovered her father, his arms crossed and his expression grim as he watched her arrival. Bud Morgan hadn't permed his hair—he'd shaved it all off. The terminal lights gleamed on his polished head, and fancy-looking sunglasses hung from a cord around his neck. The man who had worn either white dress shirts or neutral polos all his life had on a wild plaid shirt and bright orange shorts that hurt Lynn's eyes.

"Hey, babe. Showtime." Tony slipped his hand from her waist to her bottom and squeezed.

With a gasp of indignation, she turned toward him, and he swooped into a kiss, plunging his tongue into her open mouth. When she tried to struggle free, he held her head and continued the assault. Gradually, her surroundings began to fade as his tongue probed and teased, stroked and suggested. She lost her grip on her suitcase and discovered something to do with her free hand as she ran her fingers through the remembered silkiness of Tony's hair.

The rhythm of her pulse changed from the adrenaline rush of seeing her parents' new look to the insistent surge of desire for the man kissing her so thoroughly. A soft moan rose from her throat.

Tony lifted his mouth a fraction from hers. "That was...excellent," he said, his breathing uneven.

Her father's voice penetrated her fog of sensuous enjoyment. "If you've completed the tonsillectomy, Doctor, maybe we could get on our way toward Sedona."

Lynn felt the blush rising as she pulled away from Tony.

"Lynn." Her mother could get more reprimand into one syllable than anybody alive. "For heaven's sake. Show some breeding."

That made Lynn chuckle as she turned toward her mother of the lime-green fashion mistake. "Mom, Dad..." She took a deep breath. "I'd like you to meet the father of your future grandchild, Tony Russo."

"Cleanse your conscience, my friends," intoned a familiar voice.

With a feeling of foreboding, Lynn looked over to find Jeff standing on the outskirts of the group.

Tell them you're gay, Jeff mouthed. Then with a smile and a wave, he started down the terminal.

As Tony muttered an oath, Lynn glanced quickly toward her mother, a legendary reader of lips.

"Gay?" Gladys looked from Lynn to Tony. "Who's

gay? I thought you were pregnant and he was the impregnator?''

"I am. He is," Lynn said. "Forget it. Let's go."

Bud ignored his daughter and put a protective arm around Gladys's shoulders. "I wish I didn't have to be the one to tell you, Gladys, but I've learned a few things, living as I have in the soft underbelly of the city."

"Take your arm off me," Gladys said. "There's no telling where that arm has been. And I want no more of that soft-underbelly talk. It's indecent."

"Indecent?" Bud looked sad as a basset hound. "Try this one on for size. Our little girl and this...Tony person, have become what they call *bi*."

Lynn choked. "Dad, we're not! That guy—"

"By? By who?" Gladys looked completely at sea.

"AC–DC."

"Look." Tony sounded agitated. "You've got it wrong. We—"

"Isn't AC–DC one of those rock groups?" Gladys asked.

"I'm trying to tell you they're bi*sexual*, Gladys."

"Saints preserve us." With that invocation, Gladys slipped to the floor in a dead faint.

4

TONY REACTED instinctively. Dropping his duffel bag, he crouched beside Gladys and supported her head and shoulders against his knee. "Lynn, get some water," he said. At least Gladys's pulse was strong, he noted as he placed his fingers against her carotid artery.

"Take your hands off her, you pervert!" Bud squatted and tried to wrestle Gladys away from Tony. His gold chains dangled in her face as he pulled her toward him. "Gladys, dammit, did you put on another one of those strapless gut-buster things? If I've told you once, I've told you a million times—"

"Gut-buster?" Tony looked bewildered.

"We're talkin' serious underwire." Bud put a hand on his wife's midriff. "Yup, she's trussed up like a turkey. Gotta get her out of that thing so she can breathe."

"Here?" Tony croaked.

"Can't. She'd kill me."

"Uh…" Tony glanced around nervously. Quite a crowd had gathered around them.

"Here's the water," Lynn said, handing him a plastic bottle. "But all she needs is to get her bustier off and she'll be fine. She always is."

"Go clear the women's rest room," Tony said, scooping Gladys up in his arms and standing in one clean motion.

"Dad, get the bags," Lynn said as she hurried off.

Bud picked up Tony's duffel and grabbed the handle of Lynn's carry-on before running after Tony. "That was some bench press. Like a human forklift or something. Do you work out?''

''Yeah, some.'' Tony aimed for the nearest sign reading Women. Then he remembered the image he was supposed to project. ''A hard body impresses the hell out of the chicks,'' he added.

Bud's eyes narrowed. ''Hey, I forgot, I don't want you touching my wife!''

''Better let him carry her, Dad,'' Lynn called over her shoulder. ''Or you'll throw out your back, like you did the last time.'' Then she ducked into the rest room.

''Last time?'' Tony glanced at Bud. ''This happens a lot?''

''Not a lot. Five, maybe six times. When she wears her gut-buster.''

''I think I'd burn the gut-busters, Bud. Can I call you Bud?''

''No.''

''Have it your way, Dad.''

''All clear!'' Lynn called from the bathroom entrance. ''Dad, you stand guard with the luggage while Tony and I take care of this.''

''Make sure you do the unhooking, not hotshot, here.''

''I promise, Dad.''

Tony winked at him. ''Me, too, Dad.'' The look on Bud's face told Tony that he was coming across just the way he needed to. He'd seen that look on the faces of several fathers during his high-school days. He'd also noticed how protective Bud was of Gladys. These two would only need a few more nudges and they'd be back together, just the way Lynn wanted.

Inside the rest room, he lifted Gladys to the sink counter. Her bottom fit neatly in one of the sinks, while her feet in the platform shoes eased nicely into the adjoining one.

''Don't look,'' Lynn instructed, moving in beside him

and pulling her mother's tank top from the waistband of her shorts.

"Not in a million years." He supported Gladys with an arm around her shoulders and gazed up at the ceiling. He'd known this trip would involve some surprises, but he'd never pictured himself standing in the women's bathroom holding an unconscious Mrs. Morgan while Lynn took off her mother's underwear.

"You're as sexy as they come, aren't you?" muttered the woman in his arms, a challenge in her voice.

Tony glanced down but made sure he kept his attention firmly on Gladys's face. "Excuse me?"

"Just as I thought! Bedroom eyes," she said, gazing up at him. "My little girl never had a chance, did she, Romeo?"

Her evaluation that he was a predatory male out to ruin her daughter bothered him more than he'd thought it would, but it was exactly what she was supposed to think. He forced himself to give her a cocky smile.

Gladys reached up and pinched his ear.

"Hey!" He tried to resist, but she had a practiced mother-lock on his earlobe. His own mom wouldn't have been able to do it better.

She pulled his head down. "Don't count your chickens, swivel-hips. She'll marry you over my dead body."

"Turn him loose, Mom," Lynn said. "There, it's off." She pulled her mother's tank top back down. "I'm throwing it in the trash."

"No!" Gladys let go of Tony's ear and sat up, grabbing a bra cup in the process. "I paid dearly for that bustier, and it gives me Dolly Parton cleavage! I'm keeping it!"

"No. It's too small." Lynn tugged back. "Besides, what about your promise that you'd throw it away after you passed out in the bowling alley?"

"I threw that one away! This one's brand-new!"

"And you still didn't get the bigger size, did you? Let *go,* Mom."

Watching the tug-of-war, Tony rubbed his sore ear and wondered what his role was in this fracas. As the elastic garment stretched precariously between the two women, he became alarmed. Somebody could get hurt. He grabbed the middle of it and hung on tight. "Look, I don't think this is built to—"

"There are ten angry ladies outside who just came off a three-hour flight," Bud said, walking into the rest room.

"Uh-oh!" Gladys and Lynn said together, and let go of the bustier.

Two reinforced bra cups slapped Tony soundly on both cheeks.

Bud cringed. "Whoops."

Lynn spun around and looked at Tony, her eyes wide. "I'm *so* sorry. Are you—"

"I'm terrific. Let's just get out of here before somebody calls security."

"Amen." Bud pulled Gladys out of the sink. "Your butt's wet."

"And thanks to you, I'll be swinging and swaying under this tank top," Gladys retorted as she walked out the door.

Bud ran after her. "Thanks to me? I didn't strap you into that contraption."

"I wouldn't have fainted if you hadn't started talking about *bisexuality,*" Gladys said in a voice loud enough to carry several feet.

Lynn glanced up at Tony. "This is a little more bizarre than I expected. If you want to back out, I'll—"

"I'm still in. After you," he said, gesturing with the hand that still held Gladys's bustier. He glanced at the garment dangling there. As Lynn's laughter echoed against the tile walls of the bathroom, he balled up the bra and made a three-pointer into the trash can. Then he looped an arm around her shoulders and guided her out of the rest room, smiling benevolently at the crowd of hostile women outside the entrance.

LYNN WAS USED to her parents' behavior, but now she was seeing them through the eyes of a stranger. She couldn't imagine why Tony hadn't caught the next flight back to Chicago, but here he was, nuzzling her ear as they stood waiting at baggage claim for her parents' luggage. Her mother and father stood at opposite sides of the carousel, arms crossed belligerently. They alternately sent dirty looks toward Lynn and Tony and across the carousel at each other.

"You're not touching me enough," Tony murmured into her ear. "Put your hand in my back pocket."

Her pulse was already jumping from his nibbling caresses. She couldn't imagine getting more intimate. "I don't really think—"

"Would you rather run your hand down the back seam of my jeans and hold on to my thigh?"

"I'll do the pocket thing," she said quickly.

"And look at me when you slide your hand in there, like you're suggesting something very private."

She'd seen women act like that with men, but she'd never dared be so bold in public. Her heart raced. "Oh, Tony. I—"

"Don't wimp out now. Your plan is working."

"Do you think so? They're standing as far away from each other as they can get."

"Yeah, but did you notice how protective your father was when your mother fainted? You've got a real shot, here. Give them a common enemy—me."

Lynn took a deep breath and turned to look up into Tony's face as she slid her hand into his pocket. The jeans were so supple and worn she could almost imagine she was touching bare skin. The muscles of his buttocks moved beneath her touch as he shifted and turned toward her, his gaze warm. She flushed with excitement.

"You're a better actress than you think," he said softly. "I'd almost believe you were enjoying yourself."

"I'd almost believe you were, too," she murmured.

"Of course I am."

He mustn't get a crush on her, she told herself. It was too soon after his divorce. "Tony—"

"Don't jump. I'm going to put my hand inside your jacket."

"Uh, where, exactly?"

"Where a guy like me would put his hand on a woman like you."

"Wait. I—" She lost the ability to speak as he slid his hand beneath the lapel of her jacket and brushed lightly across her nipple. Slipping his hand beneath her arm, he stroked the side of her breast in long, lazy motions.

"Only a fool wouldn't be enjoying this," he said, looking into her eyes.

The ache deep within her felt embarrassingly real. This was only Tony, she told herself, and he was putting on an act. They were both putting on an act. But as she met the banked fire in his gaze while he caressed her, she wondered if they'd be able to abandon the act when no one was watching.

"Kiss me," he said. "And use your tongue. Make it obvious."

She just looked at him, her cheeks as hot as the rest of her.

"Come on, Lynn." He smiled. "Get your head in the game."

Game. That's all it was. She put her hand behind his head, stood on tiptoe and brought her open mouth against his. Using her tongue deliberately, she explored the inside of his mouth.

She was the only one who could hear his small gasp of

reaction or feel his grip on her tighten imperceptibly. His nonchalant stance didn't change, and the world might imagine he took her kiss for granted as his just due.

Pulling back slightly, she looked up at him. "How was that?"

"Not bad." His voice was husky.

"Don't get a crush on me, Tony."

"Not a chance. Kiss me like that again."

"Don't you think we're overdoing it?"

"Yes, you are overdoing it, children." Jeff put an arm around each one of them. "Cast off this deception at long last."

"Go away, Jeff," Tony said, not looking at him.

"Your parents seem like reasonable people," Jeff said.

Lynn glanced at him. "You're joking."

"Well, okay, they look like flakes, but people who are willing to take fashion chances are signaling a willingness to change on a deeper level. They may be more open to alternative lifestyles than you think."

"Excuse me, sweetheart." Tony released Lynn and shrugged off Jeff's loose embrace. Then he pointedly removed Jeff's arm from around Lynn before turning to face him. "I can't make this any plainer. Leave."

"My luggage hasn't come off the plane yet."

"Then wait for it somewhere far away from me. If you don't, I'll have you arrested for harassment. I don't want to do that, but I know a thing or two about my legal rights, and you—"

"Ah, Tony." Jeff shook his head and gazed at him through the yellow sunglasses. Then he brushed at the front of his shirt. "See that? I've brushed the hostility you're projecting right off and replaced it with white light. I'm surrounding you with white light, too, my friend."

Tony gazed at him. "Ever seen the white light in an interrogation room, Jeff?"

"Okay." Jeff backed away. "You're locked into your

reality and refuse to consider another path.'' He held up two fingers. ''Peace.''

''I'm warning you, Mr. Hotshot,'' Bud said as he walked over with a suitcase under each arm and one in each hand. ''You try to set up one of those *menageries of twa* while we're in Sedona and I'm calling the cops. I don't want to see Golden-Eye hanging around this weekend.''

''Believe me, neither do I,'' Tony said. ''Need some help with those?'' He flexed his biceps. ''I'm up to the job.''

Bud rolled his eyes and set down the suitcases. ''Why not? It'll keep your hands busy.''

''All set.'' Gladys came up behind Bud, holding a small overnight case. ''Lynn, why don't you and I handle the rental-car registration while the men deal with the suitcases.'' She took Lynn's arm and propelled her toward the car-rental counters. ''We need to have a mother-daughter talk.''

''Since we're a mother and daughter, that's about the only kind we can have, Mom.''

''You know what I mean. How far along are you?''

''Well, the way I figure it, I could make partner in—''

''Not in your law career! In your pregnancy.''

''Oh.'' Lynn kept forgetting about that part. And she hadn't anticipated that question, either. ''Three months.''

''Really? You're not showing at all.''

Lynn puffed out her stomach for her mother's benefit. ''I wouldn't say that.''

''I don't know. Looks like a bad case of gas to me. You wouldn't be making this up, now, would you?''

Lynn panicked. Her mother was about to uncover the truth and ruin the whole scheme.

Gladys grinned and put her arm around Lynn, giving her a squeeze. ''Hey, I'm kidding. I know you wouldn't lie about a thing like that. Everybody carries babies differently. I'm just jealous because at three months I was already looking chubby, and here you are sleek as an otter.''

Relief struck Lynn first, followed closely by remorse. But she *had* to do something, or her parents would get a divorce!

Her mother slipped an arm around Lynn's waist as they walked. "Okay, I have a confession to make. I hate the idea of this creep being the father, but I *love* the idea of this baby."

Lynn forced herself to concentrate on her role as a besotted woman. "Mom, don't talk like that about Tony. He's the man I love, the one I've chosen, the father of—"

"So his sperm kicked one between the goalposts. Big deal. His kind won't stick around when you're knee-deep in formula and diapers. I've worked it all out. I'm moving in with you."

"What?" This wasn't going at all as planned. "You can't do that. Your life is in Springfield with Dad, and—"

"That no-nothing? He can't even pronounce *ménage à trois.*" Gladys glanced at Lynn. "And please put my mind at ease about that fellow with the canary glasses. You and Tony aren't involved with him, are you?"

Lynn was glad to be able to tell the truth for a change. "Absolutely not, Mom. It was all a mistake. Somehow, he got the idea Tony and I were gay."

"Why would he think that?"

Lynn cleared her throat. "I can't imagine."

"Lynn, you're not telling me everything. Your right eye is twitching, and your color is high. You can tell me anything at all and not shock me. I've weathered the worst, including finding out that your father has been living in a motel with ladies of the night. I watch 'Ellen' on TV. I'm not the sheltered June Cleaver you take me to be."

Lynn glanced at her mother's electrocuted red hair, her lime-green shorts outfit and her platform shoes. "I don't think anybody would mistake you for June Cleaver, Mom."

"Maybe so. But your father seems to think he looks like that fellow from 'Star Trek,' Patrick Stewart."

Lynn managed to keep a straight face. "From the eyebrows up, I suppose. What was he thinking, shaving his head?"

"You'll have to ask him. First I knew of it was when he arrived at the airport looking like a peeled onion. Maybe it was my fault for giving him a jersey with Michael Jordan's number on it. Or this is how he decided to disguise his receding hairline."

"Great disguise."

"The man has no idea how to age gracefully." Gladys shook her head.

"What a shame." Lynn chuckled and hugged her mother. "I've missed you, Mom."

"I've missed you, too, but your job is demanding, which I completely understand. That's why I'll move in with you and take care of the baby. I hope it's a girl so we can have three generations of women in one household and celebrate the glory of being powerful females united against the oppressive patriarchy, and all that."

Lynn hated to squash this bubble of happiness for her mother, but it would be squashed, one way or another. There would be no divorce for her parents and no baby for her.

They reached the rental counter. Pulling out her reservation form, credit card and driver's license, Lynn gave them to the clerk before turning to her mother. "We can't be three generations of women united against the oppressive patriarchy, Mom. I'll be married to Tony."

"I don't *think* so," Gladys trilled, looking smug. She leaned against the counter as the rental agent completed the paperwork. "I ran into Calvin Forbes the other day," she said casually.

"Really?" Lynn hadn't thought of her old high-school boyfriend in years. "How's he doing?"

"Absolutely wonderful," her mother said, putting a hand on Lynn's arm. "He's a motivational speaker. Actually, I didn't run into him. I attended one of his Seize Your Power seminars. He asked about you."

"He's the one giving those seminars?"

"You haven't heard of him? He's getting quite well known."

"I hadn't even heard of the seminars until...recently." She decided not to mention that her father thought the seminars were partly to blame for the cemetery-plot feud. She turned back to the counter as the rental agent asked if there'd be any other drivers of the car. "Oh, Mom, I need Tony," she said, looking around for the two men and the stack of suitcases.

"No, you don't sweetie. You needed that powerful little swimmer of his because your biologic clock was ticking. Now that the eagle has landed, so to speak, you and I can—"

"No, I need him to show his driver's license to the agent so he can drive the car."

"You're paying for it but he drives?"

"We don't hassle about the money issues, Mom. That keeps life simple." She glanced around and saw Tony and her father standing a distance away with the suitcases. Tony slouched negligently against a post and collected admiring glances from passing women.

"Oh, I can see how simple it is," Gladys said. "You work and he loafs."

"Tony just hasn't found a job that makes use of his unique talents." Lynn waved a hand in the air and Tony slowly pushed himself away from the post.

"Oh, I think he has," Gladys said.

Tony sauntered toward them with a blatantly sexual stride.

"Calvin doesn't walk like that," Gladys said with disapproval in her voice.

"I'm sure he doesn't, Mom." Lynn wondered which version of Tony a woman would find when she got him into the bedroom, the conservative lawyer or the sexy rebel. Not that she intended to find out the answer to that question, of course.

"What's up, babe?" Tony asked, his eyes heavy-lidded as he gave her a once-over. "Miss me?"

"I need to get you signed up as a driver of the car."

"Sure thing, sweetface." He reached in his hip pocket for his wallet.

"I was just telling Mom that we're only six months away from the delivery date," Lynn said, figuring she'd better make sure their stories didn't conflict.

"Hmm?" Tony repocketed his wallet and looked at her. "The delivery of what, hot lips?"

Gladys elbowed Lynn in the ribs. "I told you so! He's already forgotten there's a bun in the oven."

"Oh," Tony drawled, slipping an arm around Lynn's shoulders. "*That* delivery. Did you tell your mother the names we picked out?"

"Uh...no..." Lynn gave him a warning look. They hadn't discussed this, and she thought it was dangerous to ad-lib too much.

"Well, I'm rooting for a boy, of course." Tony cupped the back of Lynn's neck and began a slow massage.

"Of course," Gladys said, her gaze stony.

He had clever fingers, Lynn thought as he worked at the knots in her neck. He could probably make a woman very happy with those fingers. Some other woman, of course.

"So if it's a boy, we'll name him Rocky," Tony said. "Rocky Balboa Russo. Now, doesn't that sound like a light heavyweight to you, Mrs. M.?"

"It certainly does," Gladys agreed, staring fixedly at Tony. "And what girl names have you picked out? Trixie? Bambi? Bubbles?"

"Those are all good, but I like Lulabelle. It has a certain ring to it, don't you think?"

"Like a Chinese gong," Gladys said.

If she let Tony massage her neck much longer, Lynn decided, she was liable to dissolve into a puddle of quivering sexual needs. "I think we're ready to take off," she said.

"What kind of wheels did you rent us?" Tony asked.

"Just what you asked for, a red Mustang convertible."

"Hot damn." Tony gave her a quick and deadly kiss that left her breathless and shaky.

She had to hope he'd revert to his old self when they were alone in the cottage. Much more of this sexy behavior on his part, and she might very well end up begging him to make love to her. And then who knows what kind of tiger she'd uncage?

5

TONY COULDN'T REMEMBER the last time he'd had this much fun. He insisted they put the top down on the convertible. Gladys complained that the wind would ruin her hair, and Bud said it was already ruined and he was all in favor of a top-down drive. While they argued about hair and lack of hair, Tony put the top down and lit up a cigarette.

He only coughed once, and then he was in the groove. In no time he was sailing down the highway, a cigarette dangling from his mouth, his shades on, one hand firmly on Lynn's thigh and the other negligently balanced against the steering wheel. He'd found a rock station and cranked it up. He was, once again, the king of cool.

Lynn had told him not to get a crush on her, but a crush was for kids. What he felt for Lynn was a very grown-up lust. The swiftness of its impact reminded him of the whirlwind romances of high school, though. Since those days, he hadn't allowed himself to react with such abandon, but the change in image had set the conservative lawyer free. He felt great.

Lynn felt even better, he thought, running his hand up and down her nylon-clad thigh. What a kick knowing that he was required to do stuff like that. Through the space between the bucket seats, Bud and Gladys were watching him like a hawk. At least Tony assumed they were watching him. Bud seemed to be, but it was difficult to tell with Gladys, because the wind tunnel created by the converti-

ble's speed pretty much turned Gladys's head into a giant
Koosh ball. It was quite a combination in the rearview mirror—Medusa and Kojak.

Tony squeezed Lynn's thigh, and she glanced over at
him, her expression hidden behind sunglasses. He smiled
at her. The high color in her cheeks could be the result of
the wind, but he didn't think so. He'd decided she was as
excited about this little game they were playing as he was.
He wondered how she'd react once they were closed into
the privacy of their own cottage...for the whole night.

The law offices of O'Keefe and Perrin seemed continents
away from this four-lane highway lifting them up into the
mountains of northern Arizona. Tony tried to remember the
last time he'd taken a vacation. Not counting his Hawaiian
honeymoon with Michelle two years ago, he had to go all
the way back to spring break during college, when he and
his buddies had done Fort Lauderdale. It was disgusting
what a drudge he'd become. Even his car was boring, a
late-model sedan.

He had no idea how this trip would turn out, and if Lynn
would become more than a friend and a colleague during
the course of the weekend. But one thing was for sure—
when he got back to Chicago, he was trading in the sedan
for a red convertible. Tony The Tomcat had been asleep
for too long.

LYNN WAS ON sensory overload. The wind in her hair, the
beat of the rock music in her ears, the mountain vistas
reeling past her window and Tony's hand on her thigh were
more stimulation than she'd had in years.

Yet the plan was working. Her parents had started the
trip holding themselves stiffly apart from each other, but
Lynn kept checking the rearview mirror, and that posture
had changed. First, Gladys nudged Bud and tipped her head
toward the front seat, where Tony was gently massaging
Lynn's thigh. The caress was having an effect on Lynn, but

it was also having the desired effect on her parents. They hated it.

Eventually, Bud and Gladys moved closer together. The wind and the rock music forced them to put their heads inches from each other in order to hold what Lynn had to guess was a war council. She had to make sure her parents' first scheme didn't work, so they'd have to create a new plan. The more plans they had to make, the more likely they'd forget their feud. Then she could agree to break up with Tony, miscarry the love child, and everything would return to normal.

Everything, that is, except her image of Tony. She'd never look at him the same way again. Even the pin-striped suit, combed-back hair and professional briefcase wouldn't disguise the bad boy sitting beside her, one hand tapping out the rhythm of a song on the steering wheel, while his other hand took liberties she'd never allowed a man in the front seat of a car.

As if she needed more to excite her senses, the first view of Sedona's red-rock spires appeared in the distance.

Tony stopped tapping on the steering wheel as the sun spotlighted the russet-colored sandstone. "Wow."

"Yeah, wow." She felt proud that she was the one to introduce him to this exotic spot. She'd only been a kid when her parents had brought her here on vacation, but she remembered being awestruck. Natural sculptures the color of a ripe peach filled the valley. Over centuries, wind and water had carved monument-like formations so magnificent that some people thought the rocks had sacred power.

She'd be satisfied if they had the power to remind her parents how much they loved each other. As Tony flipped on the turn signal and took the exit leading to Sedona, Lynn glanced in the rearview mirror again. Bud and Gladys were no longer in a huddle, but they weren't far apart, either. They both gazed around them as the road curved into red-rock country.

Tony switched off the radio. "This is amazing stuff," he said to Lynn.

"Yes." Instinctively she put her hand on top of his as he rested it on her thigh.

"Maybe we should spend our honeymoon here, too," he said.

The comment jolted her until she realized he'd pitched his voice loud enough to carry into the back seat and prod a reaction out of her parents. "That's an idea," she said. Funny how the thought teased her mind and made her think of what it would be like to be having this conversation with Tony in earnest.

A horrible thought came to her. What if she and Tony might have had a chance to build a relationship? This little escapade might ruin that chance, especially if she lost her head and became intimate with him. It would be too much, too fast, and neither of them would be able to trust their feelings, not now and not in the future. In her zeal to bring her parents back together, she might have doomed the possibility of ever connecting with Tony.

"We climbed that," Gladys said, pointing to a formation several hundred feet tall.

"No, we climbed that one over there," Bud said.

"We did not. It was that one. Don't you remember? We were the only ones around, and when we got to the top, we, uh, well, I just know which one it was, that's all."

Lynn turned in her seat and grinned at her mother, whose face was flaming. "What'd you guys do on top of that rock, Mom?"

"Nothing." Her mother grew redder. "Besides, the place was deserted."

Lynn's smile widened. "Are you saying that you two did the wild thing on top of that rock over there?" She gestured toward the formation her mother had pointed out.

"No, the one over there," Bud corrected.

"Go, Bud and Gladys!" Tony said. "I knew you guys were players!"

"Probably couldn't get away with it now," Bud said. "Look at all those people climbing around. This place has sure changed. Look at all the building going on—shopping malls, housing developments, the works."

"Well, we're not the same, either," Gladys said.

"Speak for yourself. At least I don't get my hair done at Blowtorches 'R' Us."

"At least I *have* hair. Some of us apparently bought stock in a razor company and decided—"

"Some of us look like one of the Three Stooges, and I don't think I have to tell you which Stooge, Gladys. You couldn't even *fit* all that hair into a standard coffin. Have you thought about that, Ms. Top Drawer?"

"I'll have you know, Mr. Cue Ball, that this hairstyle—"

"The cottages on Oak Creek haven't changed," Lynn interrupted. "They sent me a brochure, and it looks just the way I remember it."

"Speaking of the cottages, I have the most wonderful idea," Gladys said. "Why don't you and I take one cottage, Lynn, and give the boys the other one? It'll be just like a slumber party. We can paint our toenails and give each other facials."

"Now that presents me with a choice to be envied," Bud said. "I can either room with the wild woman of Borneo or the Italian stallion. I can hardly wait to see how this turns out."

Tony gave Lynn a look that told her in no uncertain terms that the next gesture of sickening devotion was up to her.

She looped her arm around his neck and ran her finger around the rim of his ear. He shivered beneath her touch and she couldn't help the feminine satisfaction that gave her. "I wouldn't dream of deserting my Tony The Tomcat, Mom. That was his nickname in high school. Isn't it cute?"

Bud groaned. "I'm going to be sick."

"I'm sure nobody calls him that now," Gladys said.

"She just did," Bud said. "I can hardly wait to introduce him to the guys at the union hall. They'll just love it."

"So, Lynn," Gladys said. "Are you saying that his nickname refers to his talent in—"

"Well, who cares?" Bud said quickly. "I don't give a tinker's damn if she calls him Tony the Titmouse!"

"Bud, will you stop yelling in an open car, in a swanky neighborhood, about titmouses?" Gladys said.

"That's how much you know! It's tit*mice,* Gladys!"

"Bud! People are staring!"

Lynn started to laugh. "As if," she said, laughing harder, "that's never happened to you guys before." She threw her arms in the air. "Look out, Sedona! The Morgans are back!" she bellowed.

Tony glanced at her and grinned. "Congratulations, babe. You're finally loosening up."

BY PURE LUCK, one of the two cottages Lynn had reserved turned out to be the exact one her parents had stayed in during their honeymoon. At least that's what Gladys said. The cozy little place had blooming vines hanging from the porch roof and lacy curtains at the windows. Lynn imagined her parents being overcome with sentimental memories that would transform them into lovebirds.

"This isn't it," Bud said as the four of them stood on the porch of the cottage in question and looked at Oak Creek tumbling over rocks in the streambed a few yards away. "Ours was closer to the lodge."

"This most certainly is it," Gladys said. "I remember how the trees looked along the creek."

"When were you looking at the trees? I never saw you looking at the trees."

"You might not notice trees. I always notice trees. That

big one with the dappled bark is an Arizona sycamore, and the rough-barked ones are cottonwoods.''

"These are not the same trees, Gladys. Thirty-five years ago these trees were twiglets.''

"Saplings," Gladys said, sniffing. "I don't care what you say. This is the place. The scene of the crime, as they say.''

"You got that right. Jeez, Louise.''

So much for being overcome with sentimental memories, Lynn thought. She and Tony had their work cut out for them if they were going to bring these two back together.

As if reading her thoughts, Tony lit a cigarette and cradled her against his hip. "Me and Lynn, we need to go unpack, if you know what I mean.'' He winked at Bud.

Bud glanced at Tony's duffel and Lynn's carry-on. "Shouldn't take you long. Gladys, on the other hand, will need approximately a week to unpack.''

"Oh, I think it'll take us quite a while,'' Tony said with a suggestive smile. "Don't expect to see us until it's time to eat.''

Gladys crossed her arms and glared at him. "Tell me something, Tony. It's obvious how you spend your time when Lynn's around, but I'm very curious as to how you spend your time when she's at work.''

"Yeah, that's a very good question,'' Bud said, folding his arms in the same parental gesture.

Tony took another drag on his cigarette. "Oh, me and the boys like to shoot pool or work on our cars. And if we get tired of that, there's always the option of a six-pack and ESPN. I occupy myself.''

Lynn bit the inside of her lip to keep herself from laughing. He was so convincing that she had trouble remembering that he put in fourteen-hour days and usually worked weekends, too.

Her parents exchanged a look, and Lynn's mood improved. Despite their hostility toward each other, they were plotting the overthrow of her romance, and that would take cooperation.

She snuggled against Tony. "Sometimes I watch football with him, or professional wrestling. It's a lot more fun than working on those silly legal briefs I used to bring home."

Bud and Gladys stared at her as if they were looking at an alien. "Let's unpack," they said together, and turned to go into their cottage.

"Great idea," Tony called after them.

Once they were off the porch, Lynn eased away from Tony's encircling arm. She had to start putting some distance between them, and fast. He glanced at her, but didn't comment on the action.

She felt the need to make conversation and cover up the awkwardness of the next few moments. "You're absolutely amazing," she said as they headed down a stone path leading to the cottage that would be theirs for the weekend. "I can't believe you failed drama class in high school. You're a natural-born actor."

"No, I'm not. I've just reverted to the old days. I lived that kind of life once, so I'm just running old tapes for your folks."

"Well, you're right. It's working. During the drive up here, they were definitely plotting their strategy."

"Good. I like them, Lynn. I hope they patch things up."

She glanced at him in surprise. "You really like them?"

"Sure. Why wouldn't I?"

"Because they argue about silly things, and they like to pretend they're sophisticated, but they're not, and they have a real talent for creating embarrassing scenes. I'm sure you're in for more of them before this is over."

"I'm looking forward to it. I haven't had this much fun since my senior year in high school."

They reached the steps leading to the front porch of their cottage and she paused to look around. She wasn't quite in command of herself, and she needed to buy a little time before they went inside that cottage together. "You really do like them?"

"Yup. Beneath all that feuding I sense a lot of love. They wouldn't take the trouble to fight with each other if they didn't care. It's obvious they're willing to go to any lengths to protect you, and I think there's a good chance they'll forget their differences in the process."

"I hope so." She gazed at the bubbling creek. "The setting should help, too, don't you think? All those memories, and—"

"You're stalling, Counselor."

She gave him a quick glance.

"We have to get inside before one of them comes out again and catches us admiring the view instead of—"

"You're right." Lynn started up the steps, the key in her hand. Her chest was tight with a combination of excitement and anxiety. She decided to pretend the cottage was no different from her office. She and Tony had been in her office alone together many times, even late at night, when no one else was in the building. Those days might be gone forever, though.

The cottage was nothing like her office. Romantic flourishes of chintz and lace set off the four-poster and matching dresser and rocking chair. Fresh flowers sat in vases, scenting the air and turning the small area into a lovers' bower. For her parents, it was the perfect setting. For her and Tony, it was more temptation than she needed.

She stood in the doorway and surveyed the room one more time. A big bed, a dresser, a rocking chair, a small table and two side chairs. No couch.

"Are you going in, or should I just shove the bags in around you?"

Taking a deep breath, she walked into the room and over to the curtained window. Her heart was pounding frantically. She didn't know which Tony had followed her into the cottage and closed the door behind him. Would she turn to find Tony the lawyer, or Tony the rebel?

Strong hands came to rest on her shoulders. "You're shaking like a leaf," Tony said. Slowly he turned her to face him. "Talk to me."

She let out her breath in a sigh of relief. He was the Tony she'd come to know at the office, the colleague and friend, not the bad boy who made her consider indulging in unwise behavior. "You...kind of got to me with your act," she admitted.

He grinned. "You secretly go for the reckless type, huh?"

"It's probably a holdover from the days when I wasn't allowed to even look at a guy like you. Forbidden fruit, and all that."

"But the regular Tony doesn't get your blood up?"

She wasn't so sure about that. His hands resting on her shoulders reminded her of the way he'd caressed her thigh during the ride up here, which reminded her of the talented way he could kiss, which made her start shaking again.

"Hmm." His gaze roved over her face. "Guess you don't know the answer to that one yet."

"It doesn't matter. Even if I wanted you—the lawyer, the punk, all of you—it would be a terrible idea for us to get involved."

He kneaded her shoulders gently as he looked into her eyes. "Why?"

"You know why as well as I do, after all the cases we've handled. You're recently divorced from a woman you were deeply in love with. Jumping into a new relationship would only be an attempt to replace her. You wouldn't be falling for me, but for whatever about me reminds you of her."

"You're absolutely nothing like Michelle."

She smiled. "I doubt that. We're all put together in approximately the same way."

He smiled back, his gaze steady. "So you're convinced

that whatever I'm feeling right now isn't legitimate, that I'm only on the rebound from Michelle and anyone would do?''

"Yeah, that's pretty much my conclusion.''

"Then I guess I have a case to build.''

"Tony.'' Instinctively she put her hands on the soft T-shirt that covered his muscled chest, and oh, how wonderful that felt. "Don't do this to yourself. I've put you in a situation that has sexual temptation written all over it, and it's natural that you imagine yourself attracted to me. You're too vulnerable for this, and I was caught up in my own problems and didn't consider your feelings. Let me drive you back to Phoenix. Just being in this place may be enough to get my parents back to—''

His kiss was swift and unexpected. All thoughts of noble self-sacrifice left her mind at the sensuous pleasure of his mouth on hers. As his tongue suggested all manner of scandalous behavior, she whimpered in surrender, slid her arms around his neck and aligned her body with his. He kissed her thoroughly, deeply, until she was aching with need and wriggled desperately against his solid erection.

The bedside telephone rang. Rang again. Kept ringing.

With a groan of frustration she pulled away.

He released her, his breathing heavy. "Exhibit A,'' he said. "I have no intention of going home.''

"All…all right.'' Combing back her hair with shaking fingers, she picked up the receiver. She figured the persistent caller had to be one of her parents, and she didn't have to fake the breathless greeting that indicated she'd been interrupted at a delicate moment.

"Put Romeo on,'' her father said in the same stern voice she'd heard whenever she missed curfew.

She held out the receiver to Tony.

His dark eyes were filled with heat as he looked at her. Then he took the receiver, and a transformation came over him. His stance changed to cocky, his expression to bored.

He reached for his pack of cigarettes and tapped one out. "Yo."

She was strung so tight that her laugh came out a giggle. She never giggled.

He glanced at her and smiled before he hooked a cigarette in the corner of his mouth. He snapped a match with his thumbnail and lit up as he listened to her father.

Taking a drag on his cigarette, he rolled his eyes. "Give me some time," he said. "I have a little unfinished business here, Pops."

Pops. Lynn covered her mouth to keep her father from hearing her laughter. He'd hate being called that.

"I'll be there when I'll be there," Tony said, looking in her direction and giving her a blatantly sexual once-over. "I don't like to rush a lady, if you get my drift."

Lynn shivered at the idea of a long and lazy lovemaking session with Tony. He certainly knew how to fire her imagination.

"Yeah, I'll show eventually. Bye." He hung up the phone and glanced at Lynn. "He wants me to meet him in the bar for a drink."

"And you let him think that we were—"

"We were, babe." He stubbed out his cigarette and sauntered over to her, all male, all rebel. His voice lowered, deepened. "I told him I'd be a while."

She backed up. "Oh no you don't. And stop pulling that bad-boy routine. It won't work."

"I think it works great."

"You caught me off guard. But I meant everything I said before. Getting involved would be a terrible mistake for both of us."

A knowing smile touched his mouth. "Your body's talking a different language, sugarcakes."

Lord, he was sexy. A coil of excitement tightened within her. "Don't listen," she said.

"Then don't shout." He gave her a slow, meaningful smile. "Keep your motor running, babe. I'll be back."

6

TONY WALKED into the dark-paneled bar tucked in one corner of the lodge. Bud had claimed a table far from the door and a distance away from the only other customers, a young couple holding hands and gazing at each other with adoration. Tony glanced at the couple and felt a pang of longing. He missed having those sweet interludes.

Lynn was right in one regard. He'd always figured on being married, and he'd like to be married again some day. His parents' marriage was a strong one, and despite Tony's profession, which showed him how fragile the institution was, he believed in matrimony.

Somebody out there was right for him, and he'd find her sooner or later. He missed the companionship of marriage, and this time around he intended to be a hell of a companion. For that he'd need a woman he enjoyed outside the bedroom, as well as inside it. A woman like Lynn, come to think of it.

Bud drained his beer glass and gestured toward the chair opposite him at the round wooden table. "Have a seat."

Tony turned the chair around and straddled it. The pose wasn't nearly as comfortable as sitting the normal way, but it conveyed the attitude he needed to project.

Bud gazed at him and shook his head. "Want a beer?"

"Sure."

Bud signaled the waitress.

When she arrived, Tony ordered a draft and Bud ordered

a second beer for himself. Bud didn't seem inclined to begin a conversation, so Tony lit up a cigarette.

"I hope you don't plan on doing that around the kid," Bud said.

"What kid?" Tony glanced around the bar, but there weren't any children there that he could see. "You got a rug rat hiding under your chair, Bud?"

Bud snorted in disgust. "I was referring to your kid, Einstein."

"Oh." Tony kept forgetting about the love child. It was his second slipup on that score, and he had to watch himself. "The little *bambino.*"

"Yeah. The little stranger. Was that a planned thing or a miscalculation?"

Tony had no idea what the story was on that, but he had to answer. "I never miscalculate, Dad."

"Don't call me Dad."

Tony took a pull on his cigarette. "I'll have to call you something. How about chrome-dome?"

Bud's jaw clenched. "How about *Mr.* Morgan?"

"Sorry. Not my style." Even as a rebellious teenager Tony hadn't been this rude to anyone, but Lynn wanted Bud to hate him. Judging from the look on Bud's face, Tony was succeeding beautifully.

The drinks arrived and Tony held up his glass in a salute. "Here's to your daughter, the hottest little—"

"Just drink your beer," Bud growled as his ears turned pink.

Tony obligingly took a long gulp, swallowed noisily and managed a decent belch.

"Oh, for God's sake." Bud ran a hand over his face. "I can't believe that out of the whole deck my little girl picked a joker like you."

"Just lucky, I guess. This is good beer. Oughta put lead in your pencil, Pops."

"It's your pencil I'm worried about." He reached into

his shirt pocket and pulled out a checkbook. "What would it take to get you to go scribble someplace else?"

Tony eyed the checkbook. "You're trying to buy me off?"

"You're a real genius. How much?"

"What about the little *bambino?*"

"We'll work out something—Gladys and me and Lynn."

"Does that mean you and Gladys have decided to get back together?" If so, Tony thought, then his job was over. He wasn't sure he liked that idea.

"Ha! Fat chance. Just between you and me, that cemetery plot doesn't mean a damn to me. But it's the principle of the thing, and I'm sticking to my guns."

So Tony still had some time with Lynn. "I guess I thought, when you said you and Gladys would work it out—"

"We'll work out taking care of the baby. I'll move out of the Naughty and Nice Motel, of course. That's no place for a little kid. During the day I'll take her sometimes and Gladys will take her sometimes. Lynn will take over at night."

Tony didn't remember mentioning the sex of the baby. "Uh, did Lynn say it was a girl?"

"Nope, but Gladys and I are hoping. We like girls."

Tony knew his comeback was expected. He winked. "Me, too."

"Color me surprised. Listen, just name your price, and you can catch a ride out of town tonight. And that will be the end of that."

"You'd cut me out of my baby's life?"

"That's the plan."

"You act like this was some sort of immaculate conception."

Bud nodded. "That's right. All fathers like to think that, Tony, even when they like the guy."

Tony found himself becoming upset on behalf of the baby, and on behalf of fathers in general. "But I think the baby should know her father. I shouldn't be some mystery dad."

"In your case, mystery dad works for me. How much?"

"I can't believe you're trying to bribe me to cut out on my kid."

"Hey, you can drop the act. I'm betting you've already collected from half a dozen fathers. I recognize a shake-down when I see it." He shrugged. "The truth is, I can live with this. It's only money. Lynn got a scholarship for college, so we saved the money we would have spent on her. Might as well spend it now."

"Not on me you won't." Tony pushed back from the chair, reached in his back pocket and pulled out his wallet. He threw a bill on the table. "That's for my beer. I'm not drinking booze paid for by the guy trying to take away my fatherly rights." He stormed out of the bar.

He was halfway back to the cottage before he realized that his blood was pumping as if he'd really fought for his rights as a father. He knew intellectually the baby wasn't real, but the idea that Bud would try to cut him out of his role had touched something basic. He'd leaped into the argument with a burst of anger that surprised the hell out of him.

Leaving the path, he walked through thick grass to a rock on the bank of the creek and sat down to think. Just as he'd assumed he'd be married someday, he'd assumed he'd have children, but there hadn't been any rush on that score. Or so he'd thought.

Yet look at how quickly he'd invested himself in the future of a hypothetical kid. He'd really gotten behind the concept of being a father, and he was still behind it. He almost wished he had a kid on the way, and that was plain crazy.

As he listened to the cheerful music of water skipping

over rocks, he thought of how much fun it would be to share this with a son or daughter, to sail a toy boat down the current or teach the kid to fish. Until this moment he hadn't realized how much he longed for that experience.

No doubt the pressure of building his career had pushed the longing to the back of his mind. Besides that, he'd had trouble picturing Michelle as a mother, especially after he'd begun to understand how insecure she was. Had he stayed married to her, he might have abandoned the idea of children completely. But he had no trouble imagining Lynn as a mother.

"Look, Tony, I—"

Tony glanced up to find Bud standing on the bank looking uncomfortable.

"I'm sorry about that back there," Bud said. "I thought...I thought you didn't care about the kid."

Tony realized with dismay that he'd lost his place in the script. His natural reaction to Bud's offer had raised his stock in the man's eyes, and that wasn't supposed to happen. He wasn't sure what to say next.

"Mind if I join you a minute?" Bud said.

"Help yourself. It's a public rock."

Bud grunted a bit as he lowered himself and sat beside Tony. He gazed at the water in silence for a moment. "I remember when Gladys told me she was pregnant. I was so excited I went out and bought two bowling balls."

"Yeah?" Tony really got a kick out of Bud. Two bowling balls, indeed.

"One pink and one blue, to cover all the bases," Bud continued. "The pro-shop guy told me to go with yellow, sort of a neutral that fits either boys or girls, but I said, 'No neutral for this baby, Ernie.' His name was Ernie. Ernie Babcock. Had a hell of a hook. That ball of his would just belly out on the lane—" Bud swept an arm out and Tony ducked to keep from being smacked in the face. "And then *zap!* It'd whip right into that pocket and *bam!*'' Bud slapped his fist into his palm. "Strike City."

"So, did you teach Lynn to bowl?"

Bud stared at him in surprise. "She didn't tell you? Took the junior-championship title in Springfield two years running. I think she should put the trophies in her office, but she won't, so we've still got them on the mantel."

Tony would have expected that. They probably had every triumph of Lynn's childhood displayed somewhere in their house.

"And we would have taken first in the father-daughter tournament we entered, except halfway through the second game of the final match my pants split." Bud shook his head sadly. "Never forgave myself for that. I wanted to bowl anyway. Who the hell cares if your boxers are showing if you're working on a two hundred game?"

"Absolutely."

"But she was fourteen, and you know how a girl that age gets embarrassed. Later on, though, she must've figured out how bad I felt because she had a little plaque made up that said 'Your pants might split our score in two, but nothing splits my love for you.'"

"That's a nice story."

Bud looked at Tony. "Of all the things I ever had anything to do with, Lynn's the best."

"I can see that."

"And no offense, but you're about the sorriest excuse for a son-in-law I could imagine."

Tony nodded. After all, that's what Lynn had groomed him to be.

"Still, I'm kind of glad you're not the sort of guy who would take money to leave." Bud struggled to his feet and dusted off the seat of his pants. "Gladys and I will just have to try something else. Well, I guess we'll meet at the car about six and drive into town for dinner. See you then."

Tony gazed after him with a bemused smile. Bud was

obviously still dead set against the marriage. Yet Tony had the feeling that under different circumstances—say, if Tony had happened to join Bud's bowling league—they'd be friends. And Tony would consider that a privilege.

LYNN GLANCED OUT the window and saw her father and Tony sitting together on the rock. She wasn't sure how they'd ended up there, when they were supposed to have met in the bar for a drink, but they made a touching picture sitting together bridging the generation gap. They looked surprisingly relaxed with each other. Lynn had brought a few of her boyfriends home over the years, and her father had never looked so at ease with any of them.

For the first time in her life Lynn wondered if her father had ever missed having a son. He'd always acted unconcerned about the idea, but seeing him with Tony, she wondered if he looked forward to having a son-in-law he could talk sports with, another man around to understand his point of view. Lynn loved both her parents, but she and her mother had shared certain "woman" things, and her father might have felt left out once in a while.

Watching the two men talk warmed her heart in unexpected ways, but the longer she watched the more suspicious she became. What if her father and Tony had bonded over a couple of beers, and Tony was now spilling the beans about their scheme? They did look really chummy out there. Far too chummy.

She didn't know how Tony behaved after a couple of drinks. She'd never been around him when he'd been drinking, but liquor affected some people like a truth serum, and she wasn't ready for the truth to come out just yet. If Tony wanted out of the arrangement, she'd honor that, but she wanted to keep her parents in this setting for the whole weekend. She could manage that somehow, even without Tony, as long as he didn't blow their cover completely and make her parents angry with her for lying to them.

She hurried to the bedside phone and punched in the number for her parents' cottage. "Mom? Listen, I thought I'd better warn you about something. Sometimes Tony gets a little...insecure."

"Oh, right," her mother said. "I can see that. Not."

"No, really. And when he's feeling insecure, he...tells people that he's actually a lawyer."

"And of course they believe him. He's so polished and all."

"You'd be surprised how convincing he can be. He knows all the terms from being around me, and you'd honestly think he was a lawyer if you didn't know better."

"So in addition to being a leech, he's a pathological liar?"

Lynn could see the advantages in adding a new layer of despicable behavior to Tony. "That's a very harsh way of putting it, Mom. I would say he likes to fantasize."

"And I would say he lies like a rug. What other hidden talents does this man have? Does he enjoy parading around in your underwear?"

"Only on weekends."

Her mother gasped. "I was kidding! I never dreamed that he really— Lynn, what is wrong with you, that you're attaching yourself to such a man?"

"I'm just hopelessly drawn to him, Mom." Tony would be furious if he could hear what she was implying about him, but maybe he'd never have to know about her little embellishments. "He's liberated my naughty inner child. He's taught me that there's more to life than getting ahead in my career and being a good girl. He's freeing my mind, expanding my possibilities, opening my—"

"Lynn, is he giving you drugs?"

"Oh, heavens, no." Her voice grew dreamy. "I'm on a natural high of true and enduring love."

"Lynn, get a grip! You graduated magna cum laude. You passed the bar exam the first time, with flying colors. You have a job with a very good firm in Chicago. You're smarter than this!''

"A law degree can't keep you warm at night, Mom."

"I'll buy you an electric blanket! And a dog!"

"You can't replace the electricity that runs between a woman and the mate she was destined for."

"He's giving you drugs. You've never talked that way in your life."

"I've never met a man like this before, a man glowing with the power of everlasting love."

"Okay, I know what this is. You've had a self-esteem crisis. God knows why, when your life has been a series of successes, but we can't worry about that now. Calvin says that—"

"Calvin?"

"Calvin Forbes, darling. He says that we all have weeds growing in the garden of our soul, negative beliefs about ourselves popping up like dandelions, pop, pop, pop. We have to get down and dirty and yank those little boogers out by the roots."

"Mom, Calvin always was kind of flaky."

"That's because he sees what the rest of us don't."

"That's for sure. He had a bad habit of peeking into the girls' locker room."

"Oh, heavens! He was a mere boy! He's grown and matured, and now he has vision!"

"I guess he finally got the right prescription for his contacts, then."

"Lynn, you need to take this seriously."

"About weeds."

"Exactly. I have weeds. You have weeds. I was weeding my garden when I realized I wanted to be guaranteed top position in the plot. Weed your garden, Lynn. Tony's just fertilizer for that negative self-image. Ha. That's good, if I do say so myself. Tony's a bag of bullsh— Whoops, here comes your father. Maybe he'll have something good to report.''

"Dad's back? Then please remember what I said, about the lawyer thing.''

"Don't worry, sweetie. I'm remembering everything you said. Every last word. Think weeds, dear. See you at six for dinner.''

"Right. Bye, Mom.'' She hung up the phone. "Weeds,'' she muttered. "I could have sworn Calvin flunked botany.'' She glanced at the clock and saw that she only had half an hour to freshen up before dinner, and she'd love a bath in the huge clawfoot tub. Now would be a great time for that, with Tony wandering around outside.

Pulling her carry-on into the bathroom with her, she closed the door.

Tony LOOKED at his watch and realized dinnertime was fast approaching. Rubbing a hand over his chin, he detected five o'clock shadow, and decided he'd like a shave. He'd thought about affecting the stubbled look for this gig, but he really hated the itchy feeling of a beard.

He walked up the steps to the cottage with a sense of anticipation, knowing that Lynn was there. When he'd left, things had been pretty steamed up. He walked through the door into literal clouds of steam, and through the mist he saw Lynn standing in the bathroom door wrapped in a towel.

The minute she glimpsed him, she ducked back inside the bathroom and slammed the door. Too late—he'd already caught a whiff of her flowery bath oil and a tantalizing view of silken thighs and creamy shoulders. Desire seized him in a hot, sweaty grip. He sat on the edge of the bed and wrestled with urges that couldn't—shouldn't—be let loose now. He reached for the pack of cigarettes tucked in his sleeve.

The bathroom door opened a crack and he tossed the cigarettes aside. On the other hand...

"Did...did you need to get in here?" she asked.

No, he wanted her to come out, where there was more room and a comfy bed. "I thought I might shave."

"I'm afraid the mirror's all steamed up from my bath. There's no fan or window in here. That's why I opened the door. But I'm not..."

"I noticed."

There was a pause, and he could picture her digesting that comment and the flush that would tinge her cheeks as a result. He wanted that door open, and he wanted it to stay open.

"Give me five minutes and I'll be dressed and out of here," she said. "I'll use my hair dryer to clear the mirror."

"It's too damp in there to get dressed. You'll have a hell of a time, and your clothes will stick to you." Picturing that happening nearly zapped his control. "Just come on out here and let the steam evaporate while I shave." He took a deep breath and made the promise that had to be made. "I won't take advantage of the situation."

After another pause, the door opened and she came out, a white towel wrapped securely around her torso and tucked between her breasts in that mysterious and sexy way all women seemed to know how to do. She didn't look at him as she pulled her carry-all by the handle, and something about the regal way she walked across the room wearing only a towel and pulling that bag made him wild for her.

But he'd promised. He opened his duffel, took out his shaving kit and walked into the bathroom. He used a towel to wipe the mirror over the sink, and it sort of worked. It clouded up just a little after he wiped it clean, but he could manage. Stripping off his T-shirt, he ran warm water in the sink.

"What did my father want to talk about?" she asked.

"He tried to buy me off." Tony lathered up.

"Really? How much did he offer?"

"I was supposed to name my price." Tony picked up the razor and started to bring it down across his cheek. Then he glimpsed the misty portrait in the mirror and froze in place. She stood with her back to him, but she was perfectly aligned with the mirror so that by looking in it, he could watch as she slipped off the towel and reached to the bag in front of her.

"So, did you tell him something outrageous, like a million dollars?"

He stood transfixed as she stepped into a pair of black lace panties and pulled them up over her hips. The slight mist still clinging to the mirror threw everything into a soft focus, and he'd never seen anything so beautiful and provocative in his life.

"Tony? What did you say?"

He had no idea what she was talking about. What a perfect waist she had, and the most inviting little behind. Thinking about what it would be like to caress her there, he brought the razor to his cheek. "I—uh—I told him—" Oh, God. She was turning around. In a second he'd see— "Ah!" Blood oozed from the nick on his chin.

Snatching a towel to cover herself, she stared into the bathroom. Her shocked expression told him she knew exactly what he'd been looking at and why he'd cut himself.

The mirror cleared, and he met her gaze. Red drops dotted his chin.

"You're bleeding."

It stung like the devil, but he wasn't about to admit it. "It's nothing."

"Please…"

He put down the razor, his heart pounding. They could be late for dinner.

"Please close the door," she whispered.

Holding her gaze, he reached back with his foot and gave the door a nudge. It closed slowly, and he kept looking at her until the door swung shut between them.

7

MORE THAN ANY TIME she could remember in her life, Lynn wanted a glass of wine. A bottle all to herself would be even better. She and Tony sat with her parents at an open-air Italian restaurant that overlooked Oak Creek. Across the canyon rose the brick-colored spires that beckoned to people from all over the world.

Apparently they had also beckoned to Jeff, their seatmate on the plane. Just her luck he'd chosen the same restaurant. He no longer wore yellow sunglasses. This time they were purple.

The minute Lynn glimpsed him at the far end of the balcony dining area sitting with another man, she made sure her parents took seats with their backs to Jeff's table. "Did you see him?" she whispered to Tony under cover of her parents' argument about which of the spires was Snoopy Rock.

"What did you say about never running into people you met on a plane?" Tony murmured.

Lynn opened her menu and used it as a privacy shield while she mouthed her response to Tony. "Maybe he followed us up here."

Tony copied her action and used his menu to screen his face as he turned to her. "Why would he do that?"

"Because he's been treating this like a cause of some kind. Sort of *I'm Okay and You'll Be Okay When I Get Through With You.*"

Tony slouched lower in his seat and brought the menu

up higher. "I'll bet he just likes the New Age atmosphere of Sedona. Maybe he hasn't seen us yet."

Lynn peeked around her menu and looked down the length of the balcony. "I think he's seen us."

"How can you tell?"

"He's waving."

Tony groaned.

A waitress approached the table. "Would anyone care for a drink before dinner?"

"I'll bet she knows," Gladys said. "Which one of those rocks is Snoopy?"

"Uh, I've only been working here a week, and I'm not up on all that yet," the waitress said.

"I'm telling you, Gladys, it's the one right over there, with the little boop for a nose, and another big boop for the feet. Don't you remember from when we were here before?"

"No, and I say it's the one there, with the medium-size boop for the head, a flatter boop for the tummy, sort of drawn out, and two separate boops for the feet." She caught the waitress's arm. "What's your name?"

"Suzanne."

"Well, here's Snoopy, Suzanne. Look here." She drew in the air. "Boop, b-o-o-o-p, boop, boop!"

"No, no, Gladys." Bud took the waitress's other arm. "It's like this, Suzanne. Boop, little boop, then boop, boop."

"Bud, you're crazy. It's boop, b-o-o-o-p, boop, boop!"

"Boop, little boop, boop, boop."

Tony drummed on the table as he started to sing, "Boop-boop-be-doo, rang-a-rang-a-ding-dong—"

Lynn kicked him under the table. She'd never anticipated that he'd become as much trouble as her parents. "I'd like some red wine," she said to the waitress, who seemed to have gone into shock. "A big glass of red wine."

"No she wouldn't like that," Gladys said. "She'll have ginger ale."

Lynn sat up straighter. Considering what she'd been through and what she had yet to go through, she deserved this glass of wine. "I will not have ginger ale! Mom, I've been of legal drinking age for a long time, and I—"

"And you're three months pregnant," Gladys said. "Thank goodness I'll be around to monitor things from now on, if you're going to be so casual about this baby."

"What do you mean, *around?*" Bud asked.

"I'm moving in with Lynn."

"So you're giving me the house?"

Gladys lifted her chin. "I didn't say that, now, did I?"

"Look, if you're going to be living with—"

"She's *not* going to be living with me!" Lynn said. "I—"

"So that's one ginger ale?" the waitress said.

"Yeah," Tony said, patting Lynn's knee under the table. "And a draft for me."

"White zinfandel," Gladys said. "With a twist."

Bud stared at her. "A twist of what?"

Gladys waved her hand vaguely. "Some peel or other they stick in and let float in the wine."

"Sorta like a dead fish waving in the current of Lake Michigan," Tony said, catching Bud's eye.

Lynn gave him a warning glance. He wasn't supposed to ally himself with her father.

"Oh, I sure would like that effect," Bud said with a grin. "Maybe I need a twist in my beer."

"Go ahead and make fun of it, both of you." Gladys turned to Bud. "I would have thought you'd learned about twists when you were living in the soft underbelly of the city, as you insist on telling everybody and his cousin."

"The only twists I saw were the kind that Fifi does when she's dancing around a pole."

Gladys's eyes widened. "You saw one of those shows? With the twirling tassels?"

"Except there weren't any tassels."

"Oh my God! Not even tassels! Bud Morgan, where's your sense of common decency!"

The waitress ducked her head and cleared her throat. "I have a ginger ale, a draft and a white zin with a twist."

Bud passed a hand over his face. "A draft for me, too, and I don't want anything floating in it."

"We don't generally float things in our drafts," the waitress said, clearly trying to keep a straight face. "I'll be right back with your order."

Gladys continued to stare at Bud with a horrified expression. Meanwhile, Lynn nudged Tony again as Jeff left his chair and started toward them.

Gladys leaned toward Bud. "This Fifi person. Did she have on anything at all?"

"Oh, sure, a G-string. She kept having trouble with it, though, and you know how handy I am, so she asked me to fix—"

"I don't want to hear about G-string repair and you in the same breath."

"I'll bet Tony's seen a few of those shows in his time, right, Tony?"

"A few," Tony said, earning him a more serious kick from Lynn.

"It's not that I haven't seen it all before, Gladys. I mean, they hang paintings of nude women in those art galleries you're always dragging me to. What's the big deal about a naked woman?"

"Anyone for a sweat-lodge experience?" Jeff asked, putting a hand on the back of Gladys's and Bud's chairs.

"I STILL SAY somebody should have warned me he was back there." Gladys removed the wrapper on her hamburger as they sat in a booth at McDonald's a half hour later. "I looked up, and with those purple glasses, he was like a giant bug leaning over me. Anybody would have passed out."

"Anybody wearing a gut-buster, that is," Bud said.

Lynn still couldn't believe the mayhem they'd caused at the little restaurant. She picked a french fry out of the cardboard container. "How many of those bustiers did you pack for this trip?"

"A lady doesn't discuss her underwear at dinner."

Bud took a long sip through his straw. "Half the city of Phoenix is discussing your underwear at dinner tonight, Gladys." He turned to Lynn. "Don't worry. I'll do a search and destroy when we get back to the cottage."

"You will not!" Gladys said.

"Tony will help me, I'll bet," Bud said calmly. "He's the one who has to lug you around after these episodes. He must be getting tired of that routine."

"Hey, no big deal," Tony said. "The way I look at it, I can have my mama's Italian food any day, but it's not every day I get to eat at the only McDonald's in the world with teal-colored arches. I'm gonna get me a souvenir."

"Being awfully *agreeable,* aren't we?" Lynn asked. She had a terrible suspicion that her father and Tony were starting to become friends.

"We could have stayed at the restaurant, you know," Gladys said. "The management was really very nice about the whole thing, even if they did lose a few customers over it. I tried to tell everyone it wasn't the food."

Bud laughed. "Which nobody had even thought of until you brought it up in such a loud voice. Then they headed out like rats leaving a sinking ship."

"Whatever happened to that...fellow?" Gladys asked.

"After you screamed and pitched over backward in your chair, I think he decided this town wasn't big enough for all of us, and he left," Tony said. "At least I'm hoping he left."

Gladys leaned over the table toward Tony. "He's a bad penny who's turned up from your decadent past, isn't he?"

Tony leaned forward to meet her gaze. "Mrs. M., believe me, I'd never laid eyes on that penny until we got on the plane in Chicago."

"Oh." Gladys seemed mesmerized by the eye contact. "You should have those dark-fringed peepers registered, boy. They're lethal."

"Mom." Lynn waved her hand in front of her mother's face. "Snap out of it."

Gladys looked away from Tony and glanced at her daughter. "Don't think I don't understand. I understand perfectly. That's why I have to—well, never mind."

Lynn grew nervous. "Have to what?"

"Oh, you'll find out. You'll find out soon enough."

To Tony's surprise, the four of them managed to spend a couple of hours after dinner touring the shops along the main street without causing any major disturbances along the way. He noticed Lynn was drawn to a pair of beaded earrings, blues and greens in a long dangling style much more dramatic than he'd ever seen her wear.

"Get them," he murmured as he stood with his arm around her at the jewelry counter.

"They're not really me."

"If you put them on, you might discover a side you didn't know you had." He'd continued to touch her all evening, and he'd thoroughly enjoyed the excuse to do so, but she seemed tense and on edge, unable to relax.

Lynn put the earrings back on the rack and glanced at him. "I've had enough discoveries for one day."

He knew it was a clear warning for him to back off. If she still felt that way when they were tucked into the little cottage together, then so be it. But if the tension that had existed between them the last time they were alone came back, and it was strong enough to change her mind...

"I've about had it," Bud announced finally. "Don't forget that it's later back home than it is here."

"But you're here, so you shouldn't be as tired," Gladys said.

"But I was there this morning, and I'm dead on my feet."

"But if you just got an extra two hours, you—"

"Let's go back to the cottages," Lynn said. "We'll have more time to shop tomorrow, anyway."

Tony enjoyed the anticipation of being alone with Lynn as he drove the convertible through the warm night and to the parking lot of the resort. He and Lynn said good-night to her parents and he pulled her close as they walked toward their own cottage.

"I think they're inside now," she said, easing slightly away.

"They might be watching out the window." He snuggled her back against him.

"Tony, I can just imagine what you're thinking, and it's all a mistake."

"For which one of us?" He could feel the slight tremble of her body against his.

"You, mostly." She cleared the huskiness from her throat. "You're too close to this situation to see it clearly."

"I like the view from here." He leaned down and kissed her cheek.

"This could turn into such a disaster. You think you want me, and later, when you find out it was just circumstances, you'll hate yourself."

He nuzzled her ear. "Or are you worried about me hurting you?"

"Maybe a little."

"I wouldn't do that, Lynn."

"You wouldn't want to, but in the end, if your feelings are only temporary, you'd have no choice."

They'd reached the steps and he stopped and turned her

toward him. In the moonlight she looked almost fragile, her skin pale and her eyes wide with nervousness. He didn't think there was anything temporary about the feeling that squeezed his heart.

"Michelle came over to see me last night," he said.

"She did?"

"She wanted to get back together."

"Oh." Lynn swallowed. "And...are you considering it?"

He could tell she hated the idea, which made him feel great. And now maybe she'd understand where he was coming from, and they could enjoy themselves this weekend. "No, I'm not considering it. I wasn't even slightly tempted."

"Because you're still bitter. But after that wears off, you'll—"

"Hey." He chuckled. "That was my ace, and you just trumped it, Counselor. What do I have to say to convince you I'm over Michelle?"

She gazed at him. "I don't know. But don't forget that I knew you when you were still married to her. Any fool could see how you cared about her. You sent her flowers and called every time you'd be late, and—"

"And spent less and less time at home."

"Because you were concentrating on your job! We're all like that at the firm. You were no different."

"I could be, with the right person. So could you."

She glanced away. "Don't be saying things like that. It's this place, this setup, that's playing games with your head."

"Maybe, but I'm sure having a good time." He massaged her shoulders. "And you should try to have a good time too. You've got to relax—you're all knotted up."

"Well, engineering this whole caper has taken its toll."

"Along with taking responsibility for your parents' marriage and my love life. No wonder you're all tightened up."

He smiled at her. "I know a wonderful way to work some of that tension out."

"I think a glass of wine would be a lot safer."

He gazed down at her. Maybe some wine was in order, to help her relax. "I could get you some now, and your parents would never be the wiser."

"I'm not in the mood for wine right now. But you know what I'd love?"

When she looked up at him like that, he was ready to give her the sun, moon and stars. "Name it."

"A snifter of Baileys Irish Cream. It's my favorite nightcap."

"Hey, mine, too." It happened to be true, but he would have shared a glass of motor oil with her if it would break the ice. "I'll go to the bar and bring one back for each of us. Go on inside and relax. I'll be right back."

He whistled softly as he headed up the path to the lodge. A snifter of Baileys, some soft music on the bedside radio, and things might look a little different to Lynn. She wanted to give in to her feelings, he could tell, but she had this stubborn idea that he was still in love with Michelle. There might be only one way to prove to her he wasn't, and he looked forward to making his case.

The bar was deserted except for the bartender, who seemed glad to have something to do. Soon Tony had a snifter in each hand and was on his way out the door again when it opened, nearly hitting him in the face. He stepped back, and Bud walked in.

"What's in the glasses, Romeo?" Bud asked.

"Uh...I just—"

"Baileys, isn't it? And you were taking one to Lynn, weren't you? Naughty, naughty."

"Nope," Tony said. "Both for me. I really like this stuff. Needed two of them. Yes, I did."

"You're not fooling me, kid. If anything, they're both for Lynn. It's always been her special treat." He clapped

Tony on the shoulder, nearly causing him to spill the drinks. "You, you're a beer kind of guy, but she talked you into sneaking over here to get this for her, didn't she?"

"I swear they're for me. I know she's not supposed to have it."

"In that case, it would be mean to take them back and drink them in front of her, considering she'd love some herself." He put an arm around Tony's shoulders and guided him to a table. "You can sit and drink them here, keep me company."

Tony thought quickly. He'd backed himself into a corner on this one, and unless he was superobnoxious, he might be stuck. "I thought you were wiped out, Pops. A guy your age needs his beauty rest, you know."

"You've got a point, hotshot." Bud sat down and signaled to the bartender. "Trouble is, Gladys pitched me out."

"Bodily?" Tony had met women who knew some surprising moves, and Gladys might be a martial arts expert, for all he knew.

"Nah, she just told me to leave, so I left." He reached in his shirt pocket. "I still have a key."

"That's good." Tony pictured Bud bunking in with him and Lynn. It wasn't a pretty picture.

Bud ordered a draft from the bartender, then glanced at Tony. "Sit down, slick. I'm not letting you take those glasses full of Baileys over to Lynn, and you know it. She's wrapped you around her little finger and convinced you that one little drink won't hurt. I can see where she's coming from. She's under stress on this vacation, with you being such a punk, and her being in the family way and ashamed of you and all. But while I'm around, she's off the sauce."

Tony sat down with a sigh. He'd so looked forward to sipping, and kissing, and sipping some more, and...

"You don't even have to drink that if you'd rather have a beer."

"No, I like it. Really. Like I said, these are both supposed to be for me. Lynn wouldn't take a chance with the baby."

The bartender delivered the beer and Bud picked up his glass. "Then here's to that little *bambino*."

"Here's to Lulabelle," Tony said, clicking his glass to Bud's.

Bud winced. "Gladys told me about the name choices. You're not really gonna call her that, are you?"

"Sure." Tony took his cigarettes out of his sleeve and tapped one out. "Lynn said I could pick the names, and that's what I've picked."

"Could I have one of those?"

"A smoke?"

"Yeah."

"I didn't think you indulged, Pops."

"I quit years ago, but a couple of drags won't hurt anything."

Tony offered him the pack. "Just don't go getting hooked again. I don't want that on my conscience."

"Don't worry." Bud lit up and leaned back in his chair. "I should do this more, get out and have a few beers with the boys. Come home with beer on my breath and smoke on my clothes. That would bug Gladys no end."

"That's the only reason you'd do it?"

Bud leaned forward. "Just about. I figured out a long time ago that hanging out with the guys at the bar was pretty damned boring. Gladys may be a pain in the butt, but she's always interesting. Especially when she gets stirred up about something." He took a long swig of beer and gazed at Tony through a haze of smoke. "I hate like hell to say this, hotshot, but you're kind of interesting, too."

"Hey, I'm not interesting." Tony finished the first Baileys and started on the second. "I'm a dull guy. Very dull."

"The thing is, Lynn's brought home some real duds."

"Yeah?" Tony liked hearing that kind of thing.

"Honest to God. Like they've been living on Mars, for Pete's sake. Like, for instance, what's a seven-ten split?"

Tony held up two fingers and grinned. "The big kahuna. I've picked up one in my bowling career."

"That's one more than me. But the point is, Lynn brought home this one loser, Edgar something-or-other, who didn't even know I was talking about bowling. He thought it was a type of snooty champagne. Can you beat that?"

"It's hard to beat that, Pops." Tony knew people who would be clueless about the seven-ten split, people at O'Keefe and Perrin. But in the world where he grew up, you bowled and shot pool and drank beer. Michelle had begged him not to advertise his extensive knowledge of those activities, so he'd pushed those days to the back of his mind.

"What kind of average you got?"

"I haven't been in a league for a while," Tony said. Like about fourteen years, he thought. He finished the second Baileys.

Bud motioned to the bartender for another round.

"Hey, Bud, I gotta go. Lynn's probably—"

"She's probably asleep."

No doubt, Tony thought sadly.

"Just one more drink," Bud said. "I gotta make sure Gladys is asleep, too, before I try sneaking back in. She's got deadly aim with a shoe. What kind of average did you carry when you were in a league?"

Tony remembered it as if it were yesterday. "One ninety-eight."

Bud whistled. "Damn, that's good. I'd like to have you in our Friday-night league." Then he seemed to realize what he'd just said. "Well, if things were different, of course. Right now Gladys and I just want you away from our daughter and out of our face."

The way it was said, almost apologetically, Tony couldn't take offense. "Sure."

"But I hafta tell you, Tony. If you weren't such a jerk, you could make a damn fine son-in-law." He motioned to the full snifter of Baileys. "Drink up. The night is young."

8

LYNN DIDN'T RELAX in the cottage as Tony had instructed. Instead, she paced the floor and talked to herself about how to get through the next three nights without making love to Tony. Of course he wanted to. Of course she wanted to, considering that he was turning into such a desirable, exciting, forbidden...yes, that was the key. He definitely wasn't ready for love yet, which made him forbidden fruit and so very, very...appealing.

She took a deep breath. That glass of Baileys would be most welcome. One glass would take the edge off her tension, without making her vulnerable to Tony's charms. She still wasn't sure how they'd work the bed situation. Maybe a rolled-up blanket down the middle was the answer, after all.

When he didn't come back right away, she thought about setting out to find him. No, that would make her seem too worried, too eager, too uptight—too everything she didn't want to be. Still, as time wore on she wondered if the bar didn't stock Baileys, so he'd driven into town to get some. That would be like him. Then they'd have a whole bottle available, but she mustn't have more than one small glass. Not with a man like Tony sharing her bed.

After he'd been gone long enough to drive into town and back several times, she decided to call the bar. "Did a man come in and order two Baileys?" she asked the bartender.

"Yes, ma'am. Do you want to speak to him?"

"No! You mean he's still there?"

"He met a guy on his way out and I guess they decided to have a drink together."

"Really? What does the other guy look like?"

"In his fifties, a little on the pudgy side, bald. Very bald."

"Oh." Tony had run into her father in the process of smuggling her drinks. What bad luck.

"Was one of those Baileys for you?" the bartender asked.

"Sort of. Why?"

"If it was, you'd better come over and get your own. Your friend's finished them both off and started on a third one."

"Oh." So Tony had pretended both drinks were for him, obviously. "No, I don't really want any now. But thanks for the information."

She hung up the phone and paced some more. It seemed she was destined to be a teetotaler on this trip. In the meantime, her father and Tony were having a high old time in the bar together, while she and her mother were alone in their separate cottages. Her plan was veering off track at an alarming rate.

Tony might come back feeling very amorous and uninhibited after drinking three straight glasses of Baileys. Her best defense was to be already in bed and either asleep or pretending to be. She hurried through her nighttime routine and was soon tucked under the covers, wearing both underwear and pajamas, to be on the safe side. After a glance at the clock, she switched off the light. She doubted she'd sleep a wink.

A STRANGE NOISE brought Lynn upright, and for a moment she couldn't remember where she was and wondered if maybe it was Christmas morning. No, she was in Sedona. With Tony. And her parents. She glanced at the luminous dial on the clock and discovered that she'd been asleep for two hours. And the reason she'd thought it might be Christmas morning was that carolers were outside her door.

Their song didn't have much to do with Christmas, though. She climbed out of bed, pulled on a bathrobe and shoved her feet into slippers.

"Shooby-doo, bang, bang," sang one baritone. "Shooby-doo, boop, boop, boop." Then laughter. Tony.

"Let's do Frankie," said her father, who seemed to be giggling. "You know, ol' blue eyes. He has a shooby-dooby song. 'Strangers In the Night.'"

"Why not? That's what we are, strangers in the night."

"You're no stranger." Her father hiccuped. "You're my bud."

"No, *you're* Bud. I'm Tony The Tomcat."

"Singin' on the back fence." Bud giggled some more. "Come on, Tomcat. One, two, three. Shooby-dooby-doo, doo-doo—"

Lynn flung open the door. "Doo-doo. That about describes what you two strangers in the night are in. Deep doo-doo." She put her hands on her hips.

"Hi, there, Lynny," Tony said with a grin.

"Nobody ever calls me Lynny."

"Yes, they do. I just did."

"He just did," Bud added helpfully. "We're serenading you."

"If you say so." Lynn couldn't tell which one was propping up the other, but neither of them looked as if they could stand alone. To tell them they were smashed would be to state the obvious, so she didn't bother.

"Well, here she is, the object of our quest, so we better start singin'," Tony said.

"Ooo-kay," her father agreed. "Y'know, you talk better when you're drunk. You use bigger words, like quest."

"Tha's just a little word," Tony said, holding up his thumb and forefinger to measure off an inch. "A big word would be like super...calafraga—oh, to hell with it. Let's sing. Shooby-dooby-doo, doo—''

"Did it ever occur to you two songbirds that other people at this resort might be trying to sleep?"

Tony and Bud stopped to stare at each other.

"Did it occur to you?" Bud asked Tony.

"Nope." Tony hiccuped. "Did it occur to you?"

"Nope. Let's sing. Shoo—"

"Oh, for pity's sake." Lynn stomped down the steps toward them. "Come inside, both of you."

"She must like our singing," Bud confided to Tony.

"Who wouldn't?" Tony said.

"Okay, watch those steps," Lynn warned as she wiggled between them and gripped a belt loop on the back of each pair of pants.

"'Cause that first step's a lulu," Tony said.

"Nope. Not a lulu." Bud stopped as a fit of laughter shook him. "A Lulabelle! Get it?"

"Good one, Bud!" Tony turned toward Bud and they exchanged a sloppy high five over Lynn's head.

"I can't believe this," Lynn muttered as the three of them stumbled up the steps.

"Tony can belch my name," her father said happily. "Do it, Tony."

"Don't do it, Tony," Lynn said.

"Oh, yeah, Tony. Do it."

"Okay. B-u-u-u-d!"

Lynn rolled her eyes. "Charming. Listen, we can't all fit through the door at once, so let's—*oof!*"

"Too late," Bud sang out. "Wedge-o-rama!"

This wasn't funny, Lynn told herself. Her father and Tony were now best friends, which screwed up the whole plan. This wasn't even remotely funny. It was...hysterical. She sagged with helpless laughter.

Her fit of giggles caused her to stagger slightly backward, which broke the logjam and sent both men hurtling through the door of the cottage.

"Whoa, Bessie!" called her father.

She braced herself for the crash, figuring one or both of them would fall against the furniture. Instead, she heard a couple of muffled thumps.

Trying to control her laughter, she moved gingerly into the room and peered into the semidarkness. They'd made it to the big bed and were sprawled across the width of it.

"G'night, Bud," Tony said.

"G'night, Tony."

As Lynn stood there, a hand clamped over her giggles, both men started to snore. Lynn shook her head and sighed. "Perfect. Just perfect." Tucking a key in the pocket of her bathrobe, she locked the door behind her as she left the cottage.

The cool quiet of the night calmed her as she walked beside the gurgling creek toward her mother's cottage. She glanced up into a sky packed with stars and thought what a gorgeous night it was for lovers—assuming a girl's potential lover wasn't passed out in a drunken stupor at the moment. Then she started laughing again. Tomorrow she'd think of what to do now that her plan was in shambles. Tonight she'd just enjoy the picture of her father and Tony serenading her under the stars.

She rapped on her mother's door. When she got no answer, she rapped louder, and finally had to resort to banging and calling her mother's name. With luck they wouldn't all be evicted in the morning for disturbing the peace.

A light came on inside the cottage, and soon afterward, Gladys, her hair pointing in every direction of the compass, opened the door. Her eye mask was shoved up on her forehead, making her look like a refugee from a Mardi Gras celebration gone wrong. "What are you doing out there, Lynn?"

"I need a place to sleep, Mom. I—"

"You've had a spat. Wonderful."

"No, I just—"

"Wait a minute. Let me see if your father's in the bed. I had my earplugs in and I don't know if he came home during the night or not."

"He's not there." Lynn walked into the cottage, which held the familiar scent of her mother's perfume.

"Why, no, he's not." Gladys picked up the covers and peeked under them, as if her husband could somehow be hiding at the foot of the bed. "I wonder where—"

"He and Tony are sleeping in my bed in the other cottage."

Gladys dropped the covers as if they were on fire and whirled to face Lynn. "What *are* you saying?"

Lynn started laughing again. "Oh, Mom, it's not like that. They got drunk together, came to serenade me and then passed out. It was easier to leave them both there and come over here."

Her mother put a hand to her chest and sat down on the bed. "They got drunk together? I thought Tony was with you."

"He went to the bar for a…nightcap, and ran into Dad, I guess. I fell asleep, and the next thing I knew they were outside the cottage, singing."

Gladys's mouth twitched, as if she might be holding back a grin. "Your father is definitely into his second childhood, pulling a stunt like that."

Lynn sat next to her on the bed. "It was kind of cute, to be honest. They definitely did the male-bonding thing. Tony can now belch out Dad's name."

Gladys started to laugh and clapped a hand over her mouth. "That's terrible," she said, clearing her throat. "How completely low class."

"They're going to feel like hell in the morning."

"Especially your father. He's no spring chicken anymore." She glanced at Lynn. "You gave me quite a jolt when you said they were in bed together. After all this bisexual talk, and where your father's been living lately, I—''

"Oh, Mom." Lynn put an arm around her mother and hugged her. "You know Dad better than that. He's just curious about that lifestyle, but he's not a swinger, and you know it. I'll bet the prostitutes think he's just adorable, with his conservative little habits. And I believe he fixed that G-string in the same efficient way he'd repair a lamp cord for you at home. He's just not the hanky-panky type, no matter how much he tries to pretend he is."

This time Gladys did smile. "No, he's not. And that's one of the reasons I—'' She caught herself and stopped in confusion.

"One of the reasons you love him?" Lynn finished gently. "Why don't you two just kiss and make up, Mom? You know he's the only guy for you."

"I do not know that! He's blocking my path to seizing my personal power."

"Did Calvin tell you that?"

Her mother's gaze shifted uneasily. "Not exactly. You know what? We should really get some sleep. Tomorrow's a big day."

"I doubt it. Dad and Tony will be useless. I suppose you and I could go shopping while they sleep it off, but I was thinking we'd all sort of relax tomorrow. Besides, you're changing the subject. I want to know if Calvin's motivational seminar has inspired you to find fault with Dad."

"Of course not." Gladys stood. "And if you're not ready to get some sleep, I am. As it is, I'll probably look like Bozo the Clown in the morning."

"Okay." Lynn walked around to the other side of the bed and took off her bathrobe. "But I really want to find out more about this seminar, Mom."

"You will, dear. I promise." Gladys climbed into bed

and glanced over at Lynn. "Is that the nightwear you brought for this trip?"

Lynn looked down at her sedate pajamas. "Yes, why?"

"Nothing. It's just…boring. I would have thought, considering this hot-and-heavy affair you have going on, and the kind of man Tony seems to be, that you'd have picked out something a little more tantalizing."

"Um…Tony doesn't really care about stuff like that," she said.

"Don't you believe it. All men care about stuff like that. But who am I to advise you on how to keep him interested? I want you to dump him at the first opportunity!" She snapped off the bedside light.

"I really like him, Mom." Lynn discovered she didn't have to fake that statement at all. She was quite impressed with a guy who drank himself into oblivion just so her father wouldn't think his pregnant daughter had ordered a nightcap.

"I believe you," Gladys said, "but something has been bothering me all day, and I finally figured out what it was."

"What's that?" Lynn was glad the light was off and her mother couldn't see the sudden concern in her expression. She lay staring into the dark as she waited to find out what her mother's instincts had unearthed.

"No whisker burn."

Lynn closed her eyes and silently cursed the detail she'd forgotten. She had very sensitive skin, and every time she'd had a steady boyfriend, she'd battled the pink flush of whisker burn. Her mother had the same problem, and Lynn had always known when her parents had been particularly affectionate, because her mother's cheeks and chin would be pink.

She hoped a logical explanation would occur to her as she started to speak. "Well, I—"

"I can understand why you didn't have it when you arrived," Gladys said. "You've probably been working hard so you could have this time off. But after spending the afternoon with him, your skin should be a little irritated. And I can tell he has a heavy beard.''

''We haven't had all that much time together, even here in Sedona,'' Lynn said. ''I guarantee you'll see whisker burn before the vacation's over.'' And she hoped to see it on her mother's face, as well.

''You don't have to prove anything to me,'' Gladys said. ''I just realized what it was that didn't seem to fit. I'm sure there's a perfectly logical explanation. Good night, sweetie.''

''Good night, Mom.'' Lynn couldn't sleep as she worried about what her mother had said. There was a slight doubt in her mother's mind at the moment, no matter how nonchalant she sounded. And where a slight doubt existed, a chasm of disbelief might follow, no matter how truthful Lynn had been in the past.

Lynn couldn't think of any way to erase that doubt except by appearing with whisker burn on her face. And she couldn't think of any way to get that whisker burn except by kissing Tony until they were both senseless with lust. Desire blossomed as the image of doing that rose in her mind. She didn't fall asleep for a long time.

SOME FOOL was setting off firecrackers. That was all Tony could imagine as the crisp sound, combined with the ache in his head, provided one of the worst wake-up calls he'd endured in a long time. He hadn't even gotten this drunk the night he'd found out about Michelle and Jerry.

Beside him lay Bud, his new best friend, snoring away. Tony didn't remember every detail of the previous night, but he was pretty sure that he and Bud had sworn eternal loyalty. Lynn was going to kill them both, but she'd kill Tony first because he'd ruined her careful plan to make him the most hated fiancé in captivity. B-u-u-u-d loved him like a son.

Gradually, Tony realized the sound wasn't firecrackers, but someone rapping persistently on the door. They were creating that little rhythm that was supposed to be so cute and friendly. Tap, tappy-tap-tap…tap, *tap.* He hoped to hell it wasn't Lynn knocking like that. First of all, he didn't feel like facing her yet, and second of all, only a cruel woman would tap out ''shave and a haircut'' knowing he had to have the king of all hangovers. Lynn might want to kill him, but he couldn't believe she'd be cruel about it.

He finally decided the only way to make the irritating rapping stop was to answer the door. Bud wasn't going to do it. Somebody could fire a cannon through the window without rousing Lynn's father.

With a sigh Tony crawled off the bed. He would have loved to crawl to the door, but greeting someone on all fours probably wasn't the best way to start a conversation. Running a hand through his hair and a tongue over his teeth, he opened the door.

''Hey! You must be Tony!''

Tony winced at the volume of the greeting and rubbed his eyes. Whoever this clown was, he was smiling *way* too much for this hour of the morning. Besides that, he wore a shirt that was too white and a tie that was too red. Worse than that, he was chewing gum. Tony had gone so far as to turn down clients because they insisted on chewing gum. Ever since that bleacher-cleaning episode in high school, he physically couldn't stand it.

He studied the blond guy for a moment longer and wondered how a door-to-door salesman had managed to get onto the resort grounds. He cleared his rusty throat. ''And you are?''

The guy shoved a hand toward Tony. ''Calvin Forbes. Seize Your Power.''

Tony stared at him. ''All right.'' He grabbed hold of the red necktie and pulled. ''Shove off, Calvin, before I call resort security and let them know you're hustling the guests.''

"I'm here to see Lynn.'' Calvin choked out the words.

Tony let go so fast that Calvin staggered backward. "Lynn?''

"Yes,'' Calvin straightened his tie. "Would you get her, please?''

"I can't. She's not here.''

"But on the phone, Gladys said—''

"Tony, what's all the yammering?''

Tony turned to find Bud staggering toward the door. "I'm not sure yet, but any minute I'm going to get a handle on it.''

"God, my head hurts like a sonofabi—'' Bud's mouth dropped open as he glanced out the door. "Calvin? What are you doing here?''

Calvin's mouth hung open in exact imitation. "Bud? What are you doing here?''

"What am I doing here?'' Tony muttered and turned away from the door in search of an aspirin.

"When Gladys called, she told me Lynn was with Tony,'' Calvin said.

Tony rummaged through his backpack for a bottle of aspirin and finally found it.

"Tony?'' Bud turned toward him. "Where is Lynn, anyway?''

Tony crouched beside his duffel bag and tried to remember the sequence of events. It wasn't easy with the pounding in his head. "She came outside and got us while we were singing, so she was here then.''

"Yeah,'' Bud said. "And then we all got stuck in the door, and she started laughing. What happened after that?''

Tony scratched his head and frowned. "Seems to me you and I got loose and ended up on the bed. That's the last thing I remember.''

"Me, too. She must've left. Probably went over to sleep with her mother."

Tony started to nod but quickly decided rapid head movements were a bad idea. "Probably did."

Calvin crossed his arms. "I take it liquor was involved."

Bud rubbed the top of his head. "Some." He stared at Calvin. "Gladys called you? When?"

"Yesterday. I took the red-eye out here."

"We took the red-eye, too." Tony stood and twisted off the cap of the aspirin bottle. "Didn't even have to leave the bar." He swallowed a couple of aspirin dry.

"Don't remind me," Bud said.

"Here." Tony walked over and shook a couple of aspirin into Bud's hand.

"Thanks." Bud threw the pills into his mouth and swallowed. "Let me get this straight, Calvin. Gladys asked you to come out here?"

"Yes." Calvin looked past Bud to Tony. "She said Lynn was in the middle of a self-esteem crisis. I told her she'd come to the right man."

"Uh-huh." Bud looked unimpressed.

"Lynn has always meant a great deal to me, as you know."

That got Tony's attention. "Has she, now? In what way?"

"We're close friends."

"I wouldn't put it that way," Bud said. "They had a thing going in high school, but I don't think he's seen Lynn in five, maybe six years."

"How much of a thing?" Tony was amazed to discover his gut churning with jealousy. Or maybe it was partly the hangover, but he wanted to punch this guy out in the worst way.

"A very intimate thing," Calvin said with a knowing glance.

Tony's eyes narrowed.

Bud glanced at Tony. "A very short thing."

Tony relaxed a little.

"A short but very *intense* thing," Calvin said.

Tony longed to follow his first impulse and deck the guy. "I don't like you, Calvin. That may be partly because I've got the worst hangover of my life right now, but I don't think that's the problem. I think you're the problem. How can I get you to go away?"

Calvin looked smug. "Just tell me where to find Lynn."

Tony wasn't crazy about that option. First he'd like to find out just how *intense* her association had been with this overgrown Boy Scout. "How else can I get you to go away?"

Bud sighed. "We might as well send him over there. If Gladys called him, she'll be wondering where he is. And we need some hot coffee and a shave before we face those women, anyway."

Tony compared what he must look like with Calvin's bright-as-a-new-penny presentation. He didn't come out ahead in the comparison. "Good point."

While Bud told Calvin how to find Gladys's cottage, Tony went into the bathroom and glanced at himself in the mirror. He definitely needed some repair work before he saw Lynn again.

The door to the cottage closed and Bud wandered into the bathroom to peer at Tony in the mirror.

"So who is that, really?" Tony asked.

"Better spruce yourself up real good, slick," Bud said. "I think Gladys just called in the competition."

9

LYNN HAD PLANNED to creep back to her own cottage before dawn and get a change of clothes, but jet lag and exhaustion kept her asleep until broad daylight. She awoke with a start and gazed out the window in a panic. Then she groaned and flopped back onto the pillow.

"Morning sickness?" her mother shouted, shoving up her sleep mask and propping herself on one elbow to peer at Lynn. "I think I have some crackers from the plane in my purse. I think—"

"No, Mom. I feel fine. Stop shouting."

"What? You're mumbling."

"I feel fine! Take out your earplugs!"

"Oh. Just a minute." She put the earplugs on the bedside table and turned back to Lynn. "Now, if you're not sick, what were you moaning about?"

"I meant to wake up early and sneak over to the cottage before anyone was around. Now the place is bustling and I'm stuck here in nothing but pajamas and a bathrobe."

"We'll figure something out." Gladys waved a dismissive hand. "Have you been sick?"

"Why, are you afraid you'll catch something?"

"Morning sickness! Honestly, you can't seem to remember this pregnancy for more than five minutes at a time."

"Oh, *that* kind of sick." Lynn wasn't sure if morning sickness was a requirement of being pregnant or not, so she decided to play it safe. "Oh, some. Not bad."

"And what sort of symptoms did you have?"

"The usual."

"Hmm." Her mother studied her. "It's funny, but when I look at you, I don't see a pregnant woman."

"Oh, I'm pregnant all right! Pregnant, that's me." Lynn puffed out her cheeks and patted her flat stomach. "Very pregnant. Definitely pregnant."

"Maybe I'm just finding it hard to believe that my little girl is going to have a little girl of her own."

Uh-oh. Tony must have given the kid a gender when she wasn't looking. "Did Tony mention that it was a girl?"

"No. Your father and I just decided."

"Really?" Lynn sat up. "I don't think it's biologically possible for the grandparents to determine the sex of the baby."

"It'll be a girl." Gladys patted her knee. "We've saved all your baby things, and some of those lacy dresses would look ridiculous on a boy."

"Well, then. That settles it. Obviously I'll have a girl." Lynn grinned at her mother. For a wild moment she wished she could be pregnant with a girl, just to give her mother a thrill, not to mention having an excuse to clean out the attic of the house in Springfield.

"Oh, you know what I mean."

"Yeah." The crazy thing was, she did.

"I like girls. You've been so much fun to raise that I'd love to do it all over again, at least the easy parts." She narrowed her eyes. "You've been fun until recently, anyway. Lynn, we're all alone here in this cottage. You don't have to pretend anymore. Tell me the truth—he's great for sex, but you're horrified at the prospect of having him for a husband and father, aren't you?"

"Not at all, Mom." Lynn got out of bed and wondered how she'd sneak back to the cottage without making a spectacle of herself.

"Think about it." Gladys got up and started to pace.

"Tony's not going to fit in with your colleagues at the law firm."

"Oh, he might."

"Well, even if you pull that off, sort of a reverse *My Fair Lady,* you won't fit in with his lazy, good-for-nothing friends, with their fast cars and beer. How will that be for little Stephanie, having those grease monkeys hanging around the house?"

"Lulabelle."

"Stephanie."

Lynn realized she was burning daylight standing here arguing with her mother about the name of a nonexistent grandchild. "Never mind that. How am I going to get back to my cottage?"

"Wear something of mine."

"Um...okay." Lynn was a little afraid of what that might mean, given her mother's neon green traveling outfit and the neon orange jumpsuit she'd put on for dinner the night before. "Did you bring those cream-colored slacks and black shell?"

"Goodness, I gave those away to charity weeks ago! They just shouted *old lady.*"

Lynn thought her mother's current wardrobe shouted *crazy old lady,* but she wouldn't hurt her mother's feelings for the world by saying so. Cautiously she opened the closet and peeked inside.

"Good Lord!" She closed the closet doors again. Some boutique must have had a sale on neon and Gladys had bought a rainbow's worth. Everything in the closet shimmered and glowed.

"Can you believe it?" Gladys said with a happy smile. "Your mother is ready for the millennium."

Lynn absorbed the brilliance of that smile and was contrite. "If anyone is, you are." She walked over and hugged her mother, feeling suddenly protective and tender toward this wacky, adventuresome woman who fearlessly adorned herself in the most tasteless garments in the history of fashion. "Why don't you tell me what you can spare out of your wardrobe?"

"You can have anything you want. You know that."

Lynn's eyes misted. "You're the best, Mom." With a final squeeze, she went back to do battle with the closet again.

"I think the fluorescent pink would look great with your dark hair," Gladys said, coming to stand beside her. "Yes, that's what you should wear."

Lynn took the dress out of the closet. Not only was it a hot, shimmery pink, it had enormous glittering stars all over it. "It's...um...short."

"And you have the legs for it!" Gladys shoved her toward the bathroom. "Go put it on. I may even give it to you."

"Oh, Mom, that's not—"

"You need to wear more color, Lynn. I know you can't dress like this for the office, but in your off-hours, you should put a little razzle-dazzle in your wardrobe. If those boring pajamas are any indication of your leisure wear these days, you need help. No wonder you haven't attracted anyone with pizzazz. Oh, put on a little of my makeup, too. You'll need it with that bright dress or you'll look like a corpse."

"A corpse with razzle-dazzle. I'll be out in a flash." Lynn ducked into the bathroom. A few minutes later she emerged, tugging on the hem of the dress. It must have been very tight on her mother, she thought, considering how snug it was on her much skinnier frame. And because she was taller than Gladys, the skirt barely reached the middle of her thigh.

"Stop fooling with it and stand still," Gladys instructed. She put her finger to her pursed lips. "Stunning. Just right for, well, just right."

"Just right for what, Mom? What do you have up your sleeve?"

"Nothing." Her mother widened her eyes innocently.

Lynn glanced down at the dress. It made her eyes hurt. "You don't think it's a little...*much* for eight-thirty in the morning?"

"Honey, we're at a resort! Oh, you need something on your feet." She rummaged in the closet and came out with some gold thong sandals decorated with hot-pink beads. "Wear these."

Lynn figured she might as well. The idea had been to sneak back to the cottage without making a spectacle of herself. She might have had better luck in her pajamas and bathrobe, but the die was cast now. "Thanks, Mom." She shoved her toes beneath the leather straps. "Now I'd better get going." Bundling up her nightwear, she started toward the door.

"Send your father home, would you? He'll need an extra dose of B-complex after tying one on last night. I'm going to order room service and a pot of coffee."

"Do you want to make any plans for the day?"

Her mother looked evasive. "Not quite yet, dear. Let's just see what comes up."

"Something *is* going on, isn't it?"

"Something's always going on, dear. *Life* is always going on. And you have to reach out with both hands, and seize your—"

"'Bye, Mom. You're sounding a little too gung ho for this hour of the morning." With a wave she left the cottage. Her mother not only sounded gung ho, she sounded rehearsed, as if she'd practiced in front of a mirror. As if someone had coached her in the sentiment. As if...she squinted in the bright sunlight. Oh, God. Surely her mother hadn't done such a thing. Surely she hadn't invited—

"Lynn Morgan! There you are!"

Calvin Forbes.

There was no escape. They were on the same path, he traveling away from her cottage, she traveling frantically toward it. He must have tried there first and discovered she was with Gladys.

Lynn sighed. "Hello, Calvin. My mother called you, didn't she?"

"She did, as a matter of fact." His smile seemed to have glints of light coming off it, like in old toothpaste commercials. "But that was merely serendipity. I knew we were fated to meet again on the road of life, Lynn."

"This isn't the road of life, Calvin. It's the path to my cottage."

"Don't minimize the metaphor. Life is full of significant symbols, once we learn to heed them." He stopped in front of her and gestured toward her clothes. "Take that dress, for instance."

"I'd rather not. It's—"

"When you picked that dress from the rack, you were telling the world you wanted to be a star, Lynn! But something's blocking your way to becoming a star, isn't it, Lynn?"

Apparently, part of his motivational-speaking technique was to repeat someone's name as often as possible. It was irritating, especially so early in the morning. "Something's blocking the way to my cottage, and it's you, Calvin. If you weren't standing here, I'd be back in my own room, and I'd have taken off this dress and put on something more appropriate."

"What could be more appropriate than a dress bright as the sunrise, covered with sparkling stars symbolizing the success you so richly deserve? Follow your instincts, Lynn, and Seize Your Power!"

This could only get worse, Lynn realized. Obviously her mother had called in the troops, in the form of Calvin. Maybe, considering that law school had trained her in the powers of persuasion herself, she could make a case for

Calvin's leaving on the next plane out of here. She hated to appear in public in this dress, but if she didn't act right away, Calvin might settle in for the duration.

"Listen, if you'll go down to the terrace by the creek, I think they're serving breakfast," she said. "Get us a table, and I'll meet you there in about five minutes. How does that sound?"

"Stupendous."

She cringed. Stupendous. She had to get this guy out of here, and fast. Life was complicated enough without adding Dudley Doright and his traveling motivational show to the mix. "Be right back." She edged around him and hurried toward the cottage as fast as her floppy sandals would allow. Changing clothes was a luxury she'd have to forgo, as well. This matter had Urgent stamped all over it.

As she climbed the steps, her father came out of the cottage. He grimaced and shaded his eyes against the sunlight. "What's that you're wearing?"

"Belongs to Mom."

"A little bright, isn't it?"

"Calvin says it suits me."

"You've seen him?"

"I'm afraid so."

"Your mother said something about calling him, but I didn't think she was serious."

"Looks like she was." She gazed at her father with sympathy. He looked as if he'd just been rolled down a very steep hill. "Did you have a good time last night?"

Bud massaged the bridge of his nose. "Must've. You don't end up feeling this lousy unless you had one hell of a time." He glanced at her with bloodshot eyes. "This joker isn't for you, Peanut. You can't marry a guy who'd stay up half the night drinking and acting rowdy."

Lynn smiled. "Why not? Mom did."

"And she regrets it, too."

"I wouldn't be too sure about that. She asked me to tell

you to come home. She'll give you your B-complex and order up a pot of coffee.''

''She will, huh?'' He brightened. ''That sounds good. Guess I'll be on my way, then.'' He moved past her and started down the steps.

''Oh, and another thing,'' Lynn said. ''When I told her that you and Tony had been carousing last night, she tried to pretend she didn't think it was funny, but she wanted to laugh. I could tell.''

Bud glanced back at her. ''Yeah, but she'll probably chew me out for fraternizing with the enemy.''

Lynn was afraid of that, too. ''Just tell her it was your plan to keep Tony and me apart.''

''Hey, I did keep you apart, didn't I?''

''You did.'' And she was grateful for it, of course. No telling what would have happened if her father hadn't interfered.

''I didn't really plan it, though,'' her father said.

''I won't tell if you won't.''

He grinned. ''It's a deal. By the way, where's Calvin?''

''I told him I'd meet him on the terrace in a few minutes and we'd have breakfast.''

''Tony isn't going to like that.''

Lynn cocked her head and gazed at her father. ''Do you care?''

Bud looked sheepish. ''I still say he's not for you. But he's okay, for a punk. I wouldn't mind having him on my bowling team. But as for marrying you, well, you need somebody more...high-toned.''

''Like Calvin?''

''God, no. Well, see you later, Peanut.''

''Take care, Dad.'' She watched him walk away and crossed her fingers. Unless she missed her guess, her parents were beginning to thaw toward each other. Her plan hadn't worked as smoothly as she'd hoped, but the results were encouraging.

She used her key and entered the cottage. The shower was going full blast and the bathroom door was open. She gulped. That meant Tony was in there naked. She had to let him know her plans, and then she'd leave and take care of Calvin.

Drawing a deep breath to steady her nerves, she cautiously approached the open bathroom door. "Tony?"

"Lynn?" The sound of the shower stopped immediately. "Listen, I'm sorry about last night." The swish of a shower curtain indicated he was coming out.

"You can stay in there," she said quickly. "I'm leaving right away anyway. I just wanted—"

"Don't leave." He appeared in the doorway, still dripping, with a towel tucked around his hips.

Her heart thundered in her ears. She'd never seen a sexier sight in her life. His hair was wet and curling over his forehead. Water beaded on the dark hair sprinkling his chest and calves, and he'd hurried out of the shower and quickly grabbed the towel, so he was breathing heavily. He looked for all the world as if he wanted...her.

His eyes widened as his gaze swept her from head to toe. "What—"

"Mom's dress. I didn't want to walk over here in my pajamas."

"It's, um, different." He continued to evaluate the outfit. "I kind of like it. It's not what you'd call classy, but it makes you look like a girl who enjoys a good time."

"And normally I look like the kind of girl who bores people to death?" Lynn was still stewing over what her mother had said about her wardrobe.

"No! Normally you look terrific! Gorgeous, wonderful."

She felt a little better.

"Just not very...approachable."

She bristled again. "This dress should fix that. I could probably pick out my own corner and set up for business, wearing this little number."

"Aw, Lynn. You could wear a gunnysack and you'd still look like a queen."

Her heart lurched as she gazed into his eyes. "That...was a very nice thing to say. Thank you."

"I have more to say. I screwed up last night, but I didn't know what to do when Bud caught me in the bar with two drinks in my hand. And one thing led to another, and I'm afraid...he likes me. I'm sorry, Lynn. I've sabotaged Operation Gigolo."

"Not completely. I talked to him just now, and you're right that he likes you a whole lot better. But he still doesn't think you're good enough for me."

Tony looked taken aback. "He doesn't, huh? What kind of an attitude is that to have? I even bought a round of drinks, for crying out loud! We laughed, we sang, we shared manly secrets! And I'm still not good enough for his precious daughter? What does he want me to do, stand on my hands and wiggle my—"

"Tony, get a grip! We don't want him to approve of you!"

"Oh." He grinned sheepishly. "Right. Guess I got a little carried away."

The grin, the loosely fastened towel and the generous expanse of potent male was overloading her system. Her gaze kept drifting to the dragon tattoo. It made him look a little dangerous, a little unpredictable. That excited her far too much for her own good, and his. "I'd better go. I promised to meet Calvin for breakfast on the terrace."

The grin vanished. "Oh?"

"I'm going to convince him to leave."

"Oh." The smile reappeared. "Then maybe I should come with you, to make the point even more obvious."

"Thanks, but I think I can handle Calvin better by myself."

He looked doubtful. "I sure hope so. I don't know how

much of that guy I could take. Is he your mother's idea of the perfect mate?''

"I guess." Lynn ran a hand through her hair. "She attended one of his Seize Your Power seminars, and she's really into the program. That's why she bought all these wild outfits, apparently. The first thing she seized was a fistful of neon.''

"That guy inspires me to seize a few things myself. Like his throat.''

"Oh, he's just a nerd with a makeover, Tony. It's kind of touching that he came running when my mother called him.''

Tony eyed her. "If somebody's mother called and asked me to fly in and rescue a babe like you, I'd come running, too. He's no fool.''

She felt heat warm her cheeks. "Oh, I'm sure he's not—''

"After you? Guess again. Which reminds me. Just how cozy were you two back in high school?''

She smiled at his proprietary tone of voice, almost as if he was the jealous boyfriend. "Not very. Now I really have to go.''

"So you never even kissed him?" A light of challenge burned in his dark eyes.

"I didn't say that.''

"Then—''

"This is an insane conversation, and I'm not having it with you," she said with a chuckle as she started out the door. "Mom and Dad are ordering room service for breakfast. Feel free to do the same.''

"You're going to breakfast in that dress?''

"Yup." She opened the door. "Bye, Tony.''

"Bye, Tony," Tony mimicked as the door closed after Lynn. "Sure, go ahead and prance out there in a glittery little scrap of material that barely covers your cute little

butt. See if I care. Go meet Mr. Seize Your Power for breakfast and leave me, the alleged father of your love child, with room service. Don't invite me to join you. Doesn't bother me.''

He whipped off his towel and pulled on his briefs. "The hell it doesn't," he muttered. He glared at his reflection in the bathroom mirror. "You look like a happenin' dude. How about breakfast on the terrace? You're free? Great. Consider it a date."

10

LYNN FELT conspicuous in the hot-pink dress, but it couldn't be helped. She walked over to the lodge and down to a flagstone terrace overlooking the creek. In the tradition of a French café, cream-colored market umbrellas shaded several wrought-iron tables covered in pink linen. Sunlight teased its way through cottonwood and sycamore branches to dance on the water and play across the iridescent feathers of mallards paddling against the current. Lynn longed for a different breakfast companion.

Calvin had secured a creekside table, where two places were set and goblets of ice water sat waiting. Calvin's well-dressed appearance blended nicely with the ambience, although his bright red tie clashed with the pink tablecloths. Although she wore pink, Lynn didn't think she blended with the scenery. In fact, she was afraid, judging from the glances of other diners, that she injected a jarring note.

Calvin bounced up like a jack-in-the-box, his smile wide and sparkling. "You're here at last!"

She decided to try playing his game. "Yes!"

"That's great!"

"Isn't it!"

"Let's eat!"

She started to giggle as she sat in the chair he pulled out for her.

"What's so funny?"

"You're just the most perky guy I've ever met. And

apparently without the benefit of caffeine, since I don't see any coffee on the table yet.''

"I didn't want to get wired." He unwrapped a fresh stick of gum and popped it in his mouth. "Want some?" he asked, shoving the pack toward her.

"No, thanks." She smothered a smile. If he was like this without coffee, she'd hate to see what he'd be like with it. "I'm sorry I kept you waiting."

"No problem!" He sat down and adjusted the French cuffs of his shirt so they peeked out of the sleeves of his sport coat and his gold cuff links sparkled in the sun. "Besides, it turned out somebody recognized me, which gave me a perfect opportunity to pass out a few cards. Which reminds me." He reached inside his sport coat and pulled out a slender gold case. He popped the catch and held it toward Lynn. "Take several! Pass them out to your friends."

Lynn glanced down at the ornate business cards that featured a color picture of Calvin, smiling broadly. Seize Your Power flowed across the remainder of the card in a river of gold script. Beneath that was an address, phone number, fax number and web site.

Lynn took a card to be polite. "One should be enough. I can always tell people where to get in touch with—"

"Oh, take more!" Calvin wiggled the case under her nose while he chewed his gum vigorously. "You'll be amazed at how many people need this message."

She dutifully dug out a few more cards. "You sound sort of like an evangelist."

"I studied their techniques," he said with a straight face as he snapped the card case shut and replaced it inside his jacket.

"You didn't."

"I did! I—" He glanced up as a waiter arrived. "We haven't had a chance to look at the menu," he said. "Give us a little longer, please."

"I just want coffee and toast," Lynn said.

"Nonsense! That's the shy, tentative Lynn talking. Inside you there's a star who wants eggs Benedict!"

"Inside me there's a person who never eats breakfast. The toast is a concession to you. And I have a tiny favor to ask. You're not in front of a big audience here. Just me. Could you just…tone it down a little bit? As a special favor?"

Calvin sighed and shook his head. "So you're going to be resistant. I can see this will be a tougher sell than I thought." He glanced up at the waiter. "Eggs Benedict, a side order of raspberry crepes, orange juice, a fresh-fruit compote and decaf coffee for me. Coffee and toast for the lady."

After the waiter left, Calvin leaned toward her, his blue gaze intent, his jaw working more slowly on the gum. The smell of spearmint wafted around him. "I'll try to keep myself in check, but I get so excited bringing this wonderful message to people like you, that I—"

"Like me? Calvin, I don't need a motivational lecture. I'm a successful lawyer." She took a sip of water.

"That means nothing, Lynn!" He seemed to copy her, taking a drink of his water, too.

"Gee, I thought it did. My mistake." She leaned her chin on her hand.

Sure enough, he propped his chin on his hand in exact imitation of her gesture. "Maybe you have the successful career, the luxury apartment, the BMW," he said, "but beneath that facade of success, you feel worthless, Lynn!"

She'd heard about this mirroring technique before. "What makes you think I feel worthless?" She scratched her nose. When he scratched his, she had to work to keep a straight face.

"One word, Lynn. Tony Russo."

"That's two words." She leaned to one side, just to get him to lean with her. This was sort of fun.

"Your mother is beside herself, Lynn."

"Really?" She was just about to stick her finger up her nose, just to see if he'd stick his finger up his nose, but he grasped her wrist before she could try it.

"And in her hour of need, she begged me to reawaken the star within you. To remind you that it is you, and you alone, who have control over your destiny!"

"I really don't—"

"Now I want you to repeat after me, and keep repeating it over and over to yourself a hundred, maybe a thousand times a day. *If it is to be, it is up to me!*"

"That's exactly what I told myself, dude." Tony pulled up a chair and turned it backward. He had a cigarette dangling from his lip and his rebel shades firmly in place. He straddled the chair, wedging himself between them. "And here's how it's gonna be, Cal. You're gonna take your paws off my fiancée—" He took Calvin's hand and lifted it away from Lynn's wrist. "And you're gonna keep them off. *Comprende?*" Then he took the cigarette from his mouth and blew smoke in Calvin's face.

Calvin coughed and waved at the smoke. "This is a nonsmoking area."

"Really?" Tony grinned dangerously. "You know, you must be right, because there's no ashtray." He picked up the small stack of Calvin's cards sitting in front of Lynn. "I'll have to use these." Taking a last drag on the cigarette, he ground it out in the middle of Calvin's smiling face.

"Good heavens! You'll start a fire!"

"Can't have that." Tony picked up a glass and poured some water over the smoldering stack.

Calvin gazed sadly at his ruined business cards. "I'll give you more, Lynn."

"Don't bother, sport," Tony said.

Calvin straightened his tie and cleared his throat. "I suppose you think this primitive display indicates that you're oozing with self-confidence, but in reality you're a frightened, pathetic—''

''Watch it, Cal.'' Tony's eyes glittered as he put an arm around Lynn and pulled her close. ''Keep in mind I'm the father of Lynn's baby.''

Calvin gasped and stared at Lynn. ''You're *pregnant?*''

''Mom didn't tell you?''

''No.'' Calvin's jaw clenched. ''Oh, Lynn, this is far more serious than I thought. To betray yourself to this extent!''

''Whoa.'' Tony pushed himself to his feet and rolled his shoulders. ''You just insulted the woman I love, not to mention the guy who the woman I love is nuts about, which happens to be yours truly.''

''Uh, I didn't quite get that.'' Calvin's jaw worked diligently on his gum.

''You'll get this, pal. Vamoose.''

''I'm concerned about Lynn.'' Calvin stood, too. He was as tall as Tony, but not in very good shape.

''Nope. She's no concern of yours, sport.''

Lynn became worried. ''Hey, guys. Let's not—''

''Forget breakfast, Lynn,'' Calvin said, staring into Tony's sunglasses. He smoothed back his hair, and Lynn almost laughed when she realized he'd seen his reflection in Tony's glasses and reacted accordingly. Calvin turned toward her. ''This is an emergency, and fortunately Sedona has good resources for just this kind of thing. I'll take you to a vortex so you can absorb its energy. Then maybe you'll find the strength to Seize Your—''

''Don't say it.'' Tony held up a hand as if to ward off a blow. ''Because I swear to God, if I hear that stupid theme song of yours one more time, I really am gonna have to toss you in the creek.''

''Lynn, I don't know what you're doing with this Neanderthal.''

''Oh my.'' Tony shook his head. ''There's another insult.

You shouldn'ta done that.'' He stepped toward Calvin, who backed up a few steps.

"Stop this!" Lynn gazed imploringly at Calvin. "Go back to Illinois. You'll only cause trouble here."

"The trouble's already been caused, Lynn. Allow me to lift you out of this quagmire and into the sunlight!" He thrust his forefinger into the air.

"Allow me to lift you off this terrace and into the creek." Tony lunged forward and hooked his shoulder under Calvin's midsection. As Lynn watched in horror, Tony staggered off to the creek, with Calvin yelling his head off. Wading to the middle of the stream, Tony unloaded Calvin in the water as if he were a sack of dirty laundry. Then he turned his back on Calvin and waded to the shore.

"You made me swallow my gum!"

"That's a crying shame," Tony said over his shoulder.

Calvin put up quite a ruckus as he threatened to do terrible things to Tony, but the smooth soles of his dress shoes kept slipping on the partially submerged rocks in the stream, causing him to flounder around without making any progress toward the bank.

"Come on, sugarcakes," Tony said, slipping an arm around Lynn. "Let's you and me blow this joint."

She thought it was a very good idea. Calvin's frantic splashing and cursing, and Tony's shoes squishing on the flagstone of the terrace were the only sounds as they walked through the crowd of speechless diners.

"Let's take a spin," Tony said as they walked to the resort parking lot.

She thought that was an even better idea. Calvin would get out of the creek eventually, once he understood he had to take off his shoes and socks to get a better footing. A nice long drive away from the resort would be prudent about now. "He was yelling something about pressing charges," she said. "What if he does?"

Tony grinned. "Are you kidding? After the way he harassed and embarrassed you in front of witnesses? I'd make mincemeat of him in court.''

"He doesn't know you're a lawyer.''

"If he files charges, he'll find out, but I'm guessing he won't do anything. He has an image to maintain, and it wouldn't be very good publicity for his motivational seminars if the media found out he got tossed in the creek for being obnoxious to a potential client. Once he calms down, he'll realize that.''

"I still can't believe that you, a respected member of the firm of O'Keefe and Perrin, just threw somebody into Oak Creek.''

Tony laughed. "I can't, either, but it was completely in character for the guy you're supposed to be engaged to. Tony Russo, resident punk, would never have let Calvin get away with that without doing a little damage. And God, it felt good. Just like the old days.''

"Um, are you sure that's a good thing? I mean, once you get back to Chicago, you can't be tossing unreasonable judges into Lake Michigan.''

He guided her around to the passenger side of the convertible and opened the door. "I know." He helped her inside and closed the door again. "But in the meantime, I might as well have some fun, don't you think?''

She gazed up at him. "Tony, I'm getting a little worried about you. You're having entirely too much fun.''

"Don't be worried." He pulled down his sunglasses and looked at her over the rims. "I know what I'm doing.''

WHAT HE WAS DOING at the moment, Tony decided, was getting Lynn away from all the damn distractions. Here he'd thought they'd be shacked up together in the cottage, and so far they hadn't spent so much as an hour there together.

"I'll bet you still haven't had any breakfast," he said as he drove from the resort.

"The breakfast I can live without. The coffee is what I'm dying for."

"Then we'll get that fixed. I could use a cup or two myself." He drove through the business section of Sedona but hesitated to stop at any of the restaurants there. With his luck, Jeff would show up. Then he spotted a sign for an airport. For a town this size it would be small, but most airports had coffee shops.

"The airport?" Lynn asked as he turned on the road leading up a hill. "Are you planning to get out of town?"

"Nope. But I'll bet they've got coffee, and I'll bet we won't run into a single person we know. I swear, we seem to attract nutcases. First it was Jeff the Guru and now we're dodging Super Calvin."

She laughed. "Or maybe you're ashamed to be seen with me in this dress."

He glanced at her and paused, just so she'd know this wasn't a throwaway line. "I wouldn't be ashamed to be seen with you no matter what you wore," he said quietly.

"Oh." Her cheeks turned pink. "Well, thanks."

He didn't say anything more, just let his compliment sink in a little deeper. This was why he needed to get her away from everybody else, so he'd have time to let her know how he was beginning to feel about her.

She glanced at him, drew a breath and pretended great interest in the route they were taking. "Where is this airport, on top of a mountain?"

"Could be. Never been there."

"Me, neither. I guess it must be for private planes and commuter flights, stuff like that."

"Probably. I'm glad we came up here." Tony glanced at the view opening up below them. The red rocks formed a colorful border around the verdant green valley where the town lay. "The drive's spectacular."

"Sure is." She sighed and leaned back against the headrest. "This place is so special. I hope my mom and dad are working out their differences right this minute."

"I hope so, too." Tony was afraid Calvin might be interfering with their alone time right about now, but that couldn't be helped. He wished to hell Gladys hadn't decided to bring Calvin on the scene, and he hoped the incident at the creek would motivate him to go home.

"I'll know the minute they've started making up," Lynn said.

"Why, are you psychic?"

"No, I mean when I see my mother. She'll have whisker burn on her face."

Tony chuckled. "Oh."

"In fact, she wondered why I didn't have it. We have the same sensitive skin, and whenever I've had a steady guy, she could tell we were making out because I'd be all red. She thinks it's strange that you and I are such passionate lovers but I don't have whisker burn."

Tony's pulse quickened. "I can fix that."

"Um, yeah, well...I had sort of thought, before we see them again, that we should, you know..."

"Sure." He was proud of how casual he sounded, even though his body tightened in anticipation. "Be glad to."

"Oh, look at that view!" she exclaimed.

It was something to exclaim over, he thought, with Sedona spread below them and mountains rimming the horizon. But he hoped that wasn't all that had put that tremble of emotion in her voice.

"We're on top of a mesa," she said. "That makes a lot of sense, come to think of it. It's probably the biggest flat spot around."

"Guess so." He noticed she was chattering, probably to cover an attack of nerves. That was okay. In a little while, after they had some breakfast, she'd be too busy to be nervous. He followed the signs and finally parked in front of the coffee shop that looked out on a short, businesslike runway.

"Boy, overrun that sucker and you'd be toast," Lynn said as he helped her out of the car.

"Yup."

"You know, I'm a little hungrier than I thought."

"Me, too," he said as they walked toward the coffee-shop entrance. He wasn't talking about food.

He enjoyed the meal, enjoyed watching her eat and listening to her funny stories about growing up in her parents' house. As small planes taxied down the runway and customers flowed in and out of the coffee shop, he obliged her with a few stories from his own childhood, including the spray-paint incident and his punishment of cleaning underneath the bleachers.

"After that, I just can't tolerate the smell of chewing gum," he said with a grin. "I go sort of wacko."

Lynn chuckled. "I noticed. Poor Calvin."

"Poor Calvin? The guy's a public menace! I've been thinking about what you said, that your mom took his seminar. Wasn't that about the time she started talking about divorcing your dad?"

"Yeah, Dad thinks the seminar is partly to blame. But she was bored, so she would have found some way to stir up trouble, even without Calvin to egg her on."

"Still, I'm not in the mood to cut the guy any slack."

"In case you failed to notice, you didn't."

He smiled. He wasn't planning to express remorse over what he'd done to Calvin. "More coffee?"

"No, thanks."

"Then let's be on our way." He tossed some money on the table.

She glanced at the cash. "I should get this, but I don't even have my purse. I could pay you ba—"

"Don't even consider it." He cupped her elbow and guided her out of the coffee shop. "In fact, I should reimburse you for my expenses, considering what a good time I'm having on this trip.''

"No way. I said I'd pay, and I will. If my parents get back together, it'll be worth that and more.''

He helped her into the car and walked around to the driver's side. "The thing is, I'm starting to feel like a kept man.''

"But that's perfect! You're supposed to be a gigolo.''

He started the car and backed it out of the parking space. "What's the definition of that, exactly?''

"What you said. A kept man.''

"Kept for what?''

"You know what.''

"Yeah. I just want to find out if you have the nerve to say it.''

"For sex.'' She sent him a challenging look. "Satisfied?''

"Not by a long shot, sugarcakes.'' He glanced at the flush climbing up her delicate cheeks. Too bad what he was about to do would irritate her sensitive skin, but after all, a gigolo had to earn his keep.

11

WHEN TONY PULLED the car off the road at a secluded lookout, Lynn didn't think he planned to sit and enjoy the view, especially when he started pushing buttons that rolled up the windows and brought the top up on the convertible. She glanced at him.

"Would you care to join me in the back seat, m'lady?" he asked.

"Is this for what I think it is?"

"Yup."

"We don't need to do this very long before my skin will show it."

He opened the door and got out. "We can stop whenever you say the word." Releasing the catch on the seat, he popped it forward, giving him access to the back seat.

Her heart beat so fast she felt a little light-headed. She was deliberately preparing to have a make out session with Tony, she thought as she climbed out of the car and released her seat forward so she could get in the back with him. "I haven't done anything like this for at least ten years, and even then it wasn't in broad daylight."

"Just close your eyes and pretend it's dark." He sat down, reached up to the front and pulled his door shut. "Damn, they used to make back seats a lot bigger than this."

Lynn peered in at him, hesitating on the brink of this move. She'd just kiss him for a little while and then they'd drive back to the cottages, she told herself. But she seriously doubted it was that simple. "On second thought, maybe we should—"

"Stop wasting time and come on back here with me, woman," he murmured, taking off his sunglasses and tossing them into the front seat. He gazed at her, his dark eyes intense. "Let's give your mother what she's looking for."

She gulped as a wave of desire crashed over her. Mesmerized by that look in his eyes, she stepped over the lip of the door frame, tangled her foot in the seat-belt strap and fell face first into his lap.

"Whoa. You get right to the main event, don't you?"

She struggled to her hands and knees, too embarrassed to even look at him. "I tripped."

"Aw, gee." He chuckled. "And I was hoping it was intentional."

"You may have been a wild man once upon a time, but not me—" She tried to kick the seat belt loose from her ankle and nearly lost her balance again.

"You'd make a terrible wild man. Now, a wild *woman*, that has promise. Do you need some help, there?"

"I guess." She seemed to get more tangled in the strap, not less. "Can you tell I don't do this much?"

"Yeah. Here." He leaned down and smoothly unwrapped the seat belt from around her ankle. "Hold still." Stretching across her nearly prone body, he caught the passenger-door handle and swung it shut. "Now we're set."

"No, we're not. I'm still all cattywampus. I have to get—"

"I'm trapped with a back-seat klutz." He laughed softly. "Stop struggling around before you hurt yourself. Here, I'll just slide under you, like this."

She wasn't quite sure how it happened, but suddenly he was lying on his back, his knees bent so he could fit across the seat, and she was draped across his chest, her knees on the floor, her hands braced against his shoulders. The hem of her dress had worked its way up past her pantyline.

He smiled and combed her hair back from her face. "Comfy?"

"I wouldn't use that word, exactly."

He rubbed his thumb across her lower lip. "My buddies and I used to call this Sardine Sex."

She swallowed. "But we're not going to have—"

He traced the line of her mouth. "We'll have whatever you want to have," he said softly.

"In here?" Her voice came out a squeak.

"Why not? It happens all the time." He tunneled his fingers through her hair and brushed his thumbs across her cheeks. "Did you ever?"

"Not all the way." Her heart thudded in her chest. She hadn't really thought they would...but then again...

"That's right." His gaze roamed her face. "You were a good girl."

"And you were a bad boy."

"Yeah. And back then, I would have given my whole beer bottle collection to crawl in the back seat with a classy girl like you."

"That's funny." She traced his lower lip with her finger. "I would have given my autographed picture of Bruce Springsteen to crawl in the back seat with a wild boy like you."

"And here we are," he murmured, drawing her down.

"Here we are." She waited until the last minute to close her eyes, because she loved looking at his mouth, so eager for her kiss. Of course, this was only part of the game, she told herself. She needed whisker burn to continue fooling her mother. Yet as she allowed her lips to settle softly over his, she knew that her mother was only an excuse.

He moaned low in his throat as they made contact. The intimate sound excited her even more, and she shifted her mouth to go deeper, to begin the love play with her tongue that would drive him crazy. She couldn't remember why that was a bad idea. In fact, it seemed like the best idea in the world.

She could feel the rapid thrum of his heart against her breast and the sensuous movement of his muscles as he wrapped his arms around her. Lifting slightly away from him, she caressed his soft T-shirt and felt his chest muscles bunch in response. The scent of car upholstery, the feel of his shirt, the slight taste of cigarettes, all combined to turn her fantasy of making out with a bad boy into dizzying reality.

His mouth was so supple, so tantalizing. She kissed him greedily and found that his kisses only increased her hunger.

As if reading her mind, his touch became more exploratory. Running a hand over her hip, he found the hem of her dress and pushed it up. His caress over the satin of her panties made her shiver with delight. And through it all he kept kissing her, using his clever mouth to arouse her until she was mindless with need.

Communication changed to low, indistinct murmurs and fevered groans. Heat built in the closed car until they were both slick with sweat, which only excited her more. When he grasped her hips and lifted her above him, she wanted nothing more than to wiggle closer, to mold herself to his body, to join with him in frenzied motion.

Instead, she nearly put him out of commission.

He grabbed her knee just before she placed it in his crotch. Still keeping her mouth very busy, he eased sideways and guided her until she was straddling him, her behind in the air.

"Slide down," he said against her mouth.

She did, slipping into place like a bendable toy, the soles of her feet pointing up at the roof of the car. It was a most undignified position. Ah, but the most sensitive part of her was wedged right over his erection, and that was nice. Very nice, indeed.

"Mmm." Tony wiggled against her and murmured something she couldn't understand. By now her dress was up around her waist, and Tony had slipped both hands beneath the waistband of her increasingly damp panties to stroke her bare bottom. And still he kept kissing her.

Oh, he could kiss. His fingers kneaded her soft skin as his tongue thrust into her willing mouth. Before she realized it, she'd begun rocking gently against him. The friction on that spot felt so…great, and if she just moved like…that again…yes, right…there. He grasped her hips and intensified her movements.

Oh my. She hadn't intended…but now she couldn't… stop.

He caught her cries against his mouth as convulsions rocked her. Then he held her tight against the throbbing bulge beneath his jeans, his fingers pressed into her bottom, his breathing ragged.

Quivering from the aftershocks, she leaned her damp forehead against his and gulped for air. "I didn't mean to—"

"I know." His voice sounded strained. "But I'm…glad you did."

She realized that beneath her he was still rock-hard. She looked into his face. His eyes were squeezed shut and his jaw clenched, as if he was battling mightily for control. "Oh, Tony. This isn't fair. You—"

"I'll be okay." He sounded very not-okay.

She drew herself up enough to place a tentative hand on the tightly stretched denim. "That feels painful."

"Relative pain."

She reached for his zipper. "But I could—"

"No."

"But—" A noise outside the car caught her attention. "I hear voices," she whispered. "And a car door."

Tony groaned.

Lynn adjusted her panties and started to crawl off him.

"Easy," he cautioned, breathing hard.

"I will be," she murmured. "Oops. Sorry. It's not easy, avoiding that particular area, the way it's, um, protruding."

"Uh-huh."

"Maybe they'll go away. Then I can—"

"I don't think we'll be playing any more back-seat games." His eyes were still squeezed shut and he spoke through clenched teeth. "I have the mother of all charley horses in my right leg."

"Tony! You should have said something!"

"Do you think you could call out my name a little louder? I'm not sure the folks out there heard you."

"I doubt they're even out there anymore." She stroked his cheek, figuring that much was safe. "I feel terrible about this, Tony. You should have told me about your leg."

He started to laugh, but it was a tortured sound. "I'm sure. There you are, going off like a rocket, and I tap you on the shoulder and say, 'Excuse me, but you'll have to stop. My leg hurts.' I don't think so. I'd lose my membership in the manly-man club if I did that."

"Want me to massage it?"

"Thanks, but I'd rather you didn't massage anything at the moment."

"Then you need to get out and walk it off."

"I think we'll need the Jaws of Life to pry me out of here."

"I'll help you." She reached around and opened her door. "Just let me find my sandals." She lost her balance. "Whoops!"

He caught her as she toppled forward, but her knee still grazed the fly of his jeans, bringing a fresh gasp of discomfort from him.

Kneeling on the floor of the car, she faced him. "I'm afraid to move. All I manage to do is fall on you."

He gave her a crooked smile. "Whose brilliant idea was this?"

"Yours." Thank heavens it had been, she thought. Otherwise she'd feel doubly guilty. "But you didn't know I was a back-seat klutz."

"You just didn't get enough practice when you were a teenager. And I'm not as limber as I was at eighteen. Was it my imagination, or do we have a perfectly good bed back at the cottage?"

She nearly choked and had to clear her throat before she could speak again. Making a deliberate decision to make out in the back seat was one thing. Talking about the bed at the cottage was taking deliberation to a whole new level. "We...all we intended to do was give me whisker burn. We don't really need...a bed."

His gaze was hot. "Yes, we do, and you know it."

She struggled for breath. "We do?"

"Don't be coy, Counselor. If I weren't such a gentleman, I could produce all kinds of evidence."

No doubt, she thought, considering her drenched panties and the seductive scent of arousal filling the steamy interior of the car. "But I don't think that making love to each other is in the best interests of—"

"To hell with that line of reasoning. Besides, we're halfway there." He rubbed her arms and his tone gentled. "Are you going to leave me twisting in the wind, lady?"

She gazed into his compelling, sexy eyes. She'd never faced him in a courtroom, and she could just imagine how he used those eyes to his advantage. "First we need to get out of this back-seat tangle. Then we can discuss our situation."

"Sounds like a stall to me. But you're right. We have to pry ourselves loose from the back seat."

"I'll help."

He laughed. "No, don't help. Just concentrate on getting yourself out, while I protect the topic under discussion." He cupped his hands over his crotch.

After what happened when she'd tried to find her sandals, she decided to risk stepping out barefoot. She put down one foot and discovered smooth, warm dirt beneath her toes. More confident, she put down the other foot and eased out of the car. She was in the process of pulling her dress down when she heard a familiar voice.

"Small world, isn't it?"

A colorful string of swearwords drifted from the interior of the car. Lynn turned and saw Jeff standing on a rock about ten yards away.

THE SUDDEN APPEARANCE of Jeff popped Tony out of the back seat like an ice cube from a tray.

Jeff ambled over, barefoot and shirtless. "Hey, my friend, take off your shoes, like she did. That's the way to feel the vortex energy coming up through the rocks."

Tony paced carefully back and forth, putting as much pressure as he dared on his right leg. "What vortex?"

"You don't know?"

The charley horse began to ease as he moved around in front of Jeff. "Nope. We just came up for a cup of coffee."

"Goodness, you're nervous as a cat. Take off your shoes and climb up there. It'll mellow you right out. I've just been there. Believe me, in no time you'll be transcending, just like me."

"Where is the vortex, exactly?" Lynn asked.

"Right up there." Jeff pointed to a jumble of red rocks with a flat one at the summit. "It's a male vortex."

"Male?" Lynn peered at the rocks. "There are boy vortexes and girl vortexes?"

"Vortices," Jeff corrected. "And they're—"

"It's been great seeing you again, Jeff," Tony said. "But we really have to be going. Come on, Lynn." He took her hand and started toward the car.

Lynn resisted, turning back to Jeff. "Then there's such a thing as a female vortex?" she asked, obviously fascinated.

"Sure is. Red Rock Crossing is one. It's a streambed, you see, and this is a pinnacle, sort of, and—"

"We get the idea." Tony glanced at Lynn. "You ready?" In his present condition, he didn't need to be discussing pinnacles and streambeds.

She looked amused at his agitation. "Guess so."

He helped her into the car and hobbled around to the driver's side.

"You're not going up?" Jeff sounded shocked.

"Maybe another time," Tony said, climbing into the car and starting the engine.

Jeff leaned down and tapped on Lynn's window.

"Hold it a minute," she said to Tony as she put down her window.

"You can buy a can of vortex energy at a shop in town," Jeff said earnestly. "Just go—"

"Thanks, but I don't think we're in the market for canned vortex energy," Tony said. "See you, Jeff. And I'm sure we will see you, over and over and over again."

"That's because we share the same karma. Then again, you never know what the Universe has planned. We may not meet again in this dimension."

"One can only hope," Tony said.

"Just in case, you have to tell me something, because I'm very confused. I thought you only wanted to put on a show for her parents' sake. So what were you two doing in the back seat of the car?"

Tony leaned his forearms on the steering wheel and gazed over at Jeff. "Needlepoint," he said. Then he put the car in gear and pulled out of the parking area.

Lynn glanced at Tony as they continued down the road. "So we accidentally stumbled onto a vortex."

"Looks like."

"You know, I did feel special energy on that spot, even if we weren't right on the vortex itself."

"That wasn't vortex energy, honey bunch."

She grinned. "I suppose you're going to claim credit?"

"Damn straight." He looked over at her. "And I'm afraid you do have whisker burn."

"Yup."

"Does it hurt?"

She touched her chin. "Just feels a little tender."

"I don't like the idea of doing that to you every time I kiss you. Maybe if I shave really close before—"

"Tony." She laid a hand on his arm. "I think it would be a huge mistake if we made love. You'd soon discover that, and beat yourself up for allowing the excitement of the moment to influence you."

"Or I might discover it wasn't a mistake at all."

"You're a divorce lawyer! You know the odds against a relationship taking hold so soon after a divorce!"

"When you concocted this plan to bring your parents back together, did you consider it a gamble?"

"Well, of course it's a gamble. We're dealing with people, after all, and people are unpre—" She stopped speaking and stared at him. "Oh, you're good. You're very good."

He took her hand and brought it to his lips. "Take a chance on me, Lynn."

12

LYNN HADN'T BEEN CRAZY about her outfit to begin with. After the session in the back seat with Tony, she felt bedraggled as well as conspicuous. The pulled-together lawyer had been replaced by a tousled tart. She decided if fate had any sense of decency, she'd be allowed to escape to her cottage and change clothes without running into anyone she knew.

"There you are!" Calvin erupted from her parents' doorway as they tried to sneak quietly past. "Just in time!"

Astonished, Lynn glanced up at him as he stood on the porch above them. He reminded her of a cartoon character who gets annihilated and bounces back in the next frame of the reel looking exactly as he did before the disaster. Calvin's clothes looked precisely like the ones he'd been wearing when Tony dunked him in the creek, only these were dry. His smile was firmly in place, his mouth working on a fresh stick of gum.

Calvin strode down the steps and shoved his hand in Tony's direction. "No hard feelings, okay, Tony?"

Tony looked as amazed as she was. Here they'd been speculating as to whether Calvin would sue, and instead he was offering his hand in friendship.

"Uh, no," Tony said, returning the hearty handshake. "No hard feelings, pal."

"Oh, you're just in time!" Gladys said, coming out of the cottage in an iridescent-purple tank top and shorts. "How wonderful!"

Lynn had a sinking sensation in her stomach that something was about to happen and she wasn't going to like it. "In time for what, Mom?"

"Why, the Jeep tour, of course." Gladys hurried down the steps and put a hand on Calvin's arm. "Dear Calvin reserved space for five, just in case you two arrived in time."

Lynn looked at Tony and saw the dismay in his eyes. A Jeep tour with her parents and Calvin probably didn't appeal to him any more than it did to her. "Um, well, I—"

"Hey, Peanut." Her father came out of the cottage wearing his favorite Chicago Bulls cap. "I'm glad you made it. Remember the Jeep tour we took when we came here as a family years ago?"

"Yes, but—"

"We remembered how much you loved that, so we thought it would be a real treat to go again. Then I was afraid you wouldn't get back in time, but here you are."

"Yup, here I am." She squeezed Tony's hand and gave him a look of sympathy. "But you don't have to come along, sweetheart, if you're too tired."

"Good call, Lynn!" Calvin frowned in apparent concern as he studied Tony. "This guy looks whipped. I even noticed him limping as you walked up. He's done in. Drained of all energy! Completely—"

"Cool your jets, Forbes. As it happens, I feel like a million bucks." Tony flexed his muscles and sent a warning glance Calvin's way.

"I would have guessed a much smaller amount." Calvin shrugged. "But have it your way."

"I plan to," Tony said, slipping an arm around Lynn.

Wonderful, Lynn thought. She'd get to spend the afternoon with a pair of rutting bull elks. But once she'd seen that hopeful look in her father's eyes, she'd realized she had to go on this tour. She turned to her mother. "I'd like to freshen up first."

"No time," Gladys said. "We're due there in ten minutes. You look fine. That dress is the kind that doesn't wrinkle, even if you sleep in it." She peered more closely at Lynn. "Which might be a more accurate remark than I meant to make."

Tony gave Lynn a possessive squeeze. "Just watermelon juice, Mrs. M. We found a roadside stand and made pigs of ourselves. Then we drove all over the place with the top down on the convertible, which is how her hair got so mussed up. Had a great time, though."

Gladys looked surprised by Tony's story. "Very gallant. I don't believe a word of it, but it's a gentlemanly gesture, nevertheless. Considering what happened down at the creek, I wouldn't have expected it."

"Now, Gladys." Calvin turned to her, his manner smooth as aged bourbon. "We all agreed not to bring that up, remember?"

"I didn't bring it up. I made a passing reference. That's not the same as bringing it up."

"Well, we can all just forget about anything negative from now on, right, Tony?" Calvin slapped Tony on the back.

"Absolutely, Calvin!" Tony whacked Calvin on the back so hard his gum flew from his mouth.

Five pairs of eyes followed the arc of its flight until it plopped down the front of Gladys's tank top.

As if by reflex, she smacked her hand where it had landed. Then her eyes widened as she experienced the aftereffect. "Eew," she said, grimacing.

Calvin started forward, as if to remedy the situation. "Here. Let me—"

"Back off, hotshot," Bud said. "You'll never chew that wad again, anyhow."

Calvin gasped. "I wouldn't put it back in my mouth!"

Tony grinned. "So you say."

"Look, Russo, I'm trying to be civil. You could do the same."

Tony's grin widened. "I don't see what's so civil about spitting your gum down Mrs. M.'s blouse."

"Okay, kids, Gladys and I are going inside to take care of this," Bud said. "I don't want any funny business while we're gone. We'll be back in two minutes."

Gladys started up the steps. "You stay here, Bud. I can take care of this."

"It'll go faster if I help you."

"Oh, all right. If you must, you must."

Bud followed her to the door and turned before going inside. "And I'd better not find any problems when we get back."

Tony and Calvin stood glaring at each other and not speaking.

"This is all your fault, you know," Calvin finally said.

Tony lit up a cigarette. "You started the backslapping routine, pal."

"I slapped you on the back like a friend."

"Oh, sure. We're so close, you and me."

"That's the way the gesture was intended. With goodwill. Then you practically knocked me flat."

"Deary me." Tony took a long drag on his cigarette. "Guess I don't know my own strength." He blew smoke in Calvin's direction.

Calvin waved it away and coughed. "What a disgusting habit."

"It's better than putting a strip of rubberized candy in your mouth and chewing away like Bossie. And even Bossie doesn't spit her cud out into some unsuspecting woman's cleavage."

"I wouldn't have done that if you hadn't—"

"Hey." Lynn put a hand on each of their arms. "You know what? I'm *glad* this happened. In fact, I'm thrilled to death."

"You're glad your mother has gum mashed into her bra?" Tony asked.

Tony and Calvin both stared at her as if she'd lost her marbles.

"Aren't you paying attention? My dad offered to help her with the problem, and she's letting him do it! Furthermore, they said they'd be back in two minutes, and it's way past that."

"So they're having trouble with it," Tony said. "Which doesn't surprise me. Ever tried to clean gum off of something, Forbes?"

"You act like I deliberately shoved it down her front."

"Not far from it, pal! And now she—"

"They're not having trouble," Lynn said, her voice quivering with growing excitement. "You both know how they argue. We'd hear them clear out here if they were arguing."

"So if they're not arguing, what's taking them so long?" Calvin glanced at his watch. "We're going to miss that tour."

Tony looked at Lynn. "So you think this might have been the icebreaker they needed?"

"Maybe."

"Icebreaker?" Calvin asked. "What icebreaker?"

"Never mind, nerd," Tony said, gazing at Lynn. "I sure hope you're right, babe."

"Now, see," Calvin said. "Calling her *babe* is a perfect indication of how you're undermining—"

"Shall we go?" called her mother from the doorway of the cottage. She and Bud came out looking flustered and secretive. Her mother had on a yellow tank top with the purple shorts, and she was sporting the faint beginnings of whisker burn.

Wanting to shout for joy, Lynn squeezed Tony's hand, and he squeezed back. She didn't dare celebrate yet, but at least she had hope that her plan would work. Obnoxious as

Calvin was, she had him to thank, as well as Tony. At some point she'd find an opportunity to do that.

"We called the tour place and they have another one going out in a few minutes," Gladys said. "Somebody canceled, so they can just squeeze us in if we hurry. Let's go."

"Sounds cozy," Tony said, pulling Lynn tight against his hip as they all started for the parking lot. Then he leaned down and whispered in her ear, "But not as cozy as where I'd hoped to be by now."

Sexual awareness skittered up and down her spine. They might be headed off on a Jeep tour, and after that they'd probably be expected to have dinner with her parents and Calvin. But eventually, inevitably, they would be alone. And she'd have a decision to make.

HER PARENTS' CEASE-FIRE didn't last long. No sooner had the Jeep tour begun than they renewed the Snoopy Rock debate and were vigorously boop-booping at each other. And as Lynn had expected, each time the Jeep driver unloaded everyone for picture-taking and then herded them back into the Jeep, Calvin and Tony jockeyed for position next to Lynn as if they were playing musical chairs. By the end of the tour she felt like a picked-over item on the sale table at Marshall Fields.

They stopped for dinner in town. Lynn ended up, as she might have predicted, sitting between Calvin and Tony, who each scooted their chairs so close that she eventually had to elbow herself a larger space.

At last, long after a brilliant sunset had given way to an inky sky decorated with stars, they headed to the resort in Calvin's rented Lincoln Town Car. Calvin played the tape from his latest seminar all the way home. He'd tried to get Lynn to ride in the front seat with him, but she'd insisted on putting her mother up there while she sat in back with her father on one side and Tony on the other. Her father had plenty of room because Tony kept her firmly wedged against him for the trip back.

Several times during the afternoon and evening she'd caught Tony glancing at her with barely disguised hunger. Whenever she thought he wouldn't notice, she'd studied him, remembering how he'd looked wearing only a towel, wondering how he'd look without the towel, and if she dared find out. She'd gazed at his hands, and her imagination kicked into gear as to what those hands might be capable of. Many times he'd caught her staring at him, and sent her a secret smile of understanding that had rocked her to her toes.

When they pulled into the resort parking lot, Calvin turned off the engine. "Who's ready for a nightcap in the bar?" he asked brightly.

Bud cleared his throat. "Been there, done that." He opened the car door, activating the dome light.

"I'm really exhausted, Calvin," Gladys said, getting out of the car. "I'm so sorry. But perhaps you three young people—"

"Love to, can't make it," Tony said.

"Lynn?" Calvin asked, turning toward the back seat. "I know you can't drink alcohol, but perhaps a mug of hot chocolate would go good right now."

Tony traced his finger lightly up and down her arm.

She felt kind of sorry for poor Calvin, and if she had a drink with him, she could put off the moment of truth with Tony. Had they been able to escape to their cottage earlier today, she might have been swept away by the moment. But she'd had hours to consider her decision, and she was afraid making love to Tony would only bring them both heartache.

Then she became aware of her mother waiting outside the car, no doubt listening for her answer. Lynn knew she had to keep the heat on so that her parents would continue to have a common enemy in Tony. Once she and Tony were alone she could have a reasoned discussion with him and convince him they shouldn't risk their hearts at this vulnerable time. They could behave like rational adults and remain friends. Be that as it may, she still had to let her mother think she was about to have an orgy with Tony in that cottage.

She snuggled against him and put her hand on his thigh. The soft denim and the muscled leg beneath it reminded her of their session in the car this morning, and warmth curled in her stomach. She'd deal with that later. "I'm sorry, Calvin, but it's time for me to spend some quality time with my fiancé. We've had very little time alone."

She tamped down the desire that surged through her as she stroked Tony's thigh and smiled up at him. She was probably the only one who heard his quick intake of breath, the only one who realized how she'd jolted him with her touch.

Tony's dark gaze focused intently on hers. "Oh, babe," he whispered softly. Then he glanced at Calvin. "Better luck next time, sport," he said easily as he opened the door and flashed a victory smile at his rival.

A murderous light flickered briefly in Calvin's eyes. Then his usual jovial mask slipped into place. "Oh, I don't trust to luck, Tony! Personal power isn't a matter of luck, my friend. Lynn, if you change your mind, I'll be in the bar. Remember, we are the result of the choices we make. We must take time to reflect on our choices, pull the weeds from our personal garden, because one day we'll stop to realize that we—"

"Beep!" Tony placed his cupped hand over his mouth. "We interrupt this program for a test of the Emergency Broadcasting System. Remember, this is only a test." As he hummed a high-pitched tone he grabbed Lynn's hand and pulled her out of the car. Then he started at a rapid pace toward their cottage.

"Good night, Lynn!" her mother called after them.

Half running to keep up with Tony's ground-eating strides, she called over her shoulder, "Good night, Mom! Good night, Dad!"

"Good night, Peanut! Good night, Tony!"

Tony didn't slow his pace. "Good night, B-u-u-u-d!"

Lynn scurried after him. "Tony, I can't—I'm about to lose these sandals!"

"Oh. Sorry, Cinderella." He stopped so abruptly that she ran into him. Before she could catch her breath, he'd scooped her up in his arms.

"You don't have to carry me," she protested. "I just wanted you to slow down."

"Can't. Gotta get home, glass slippers and all, before you turn into a pumpkin."

She didn't have much trouble figuring out what he meant. She lowered her voice. "Listen, I was putting on a show for their benefit."

"And you turned me on in the process. Just your luck."

"Even if I did, we need to consider all this very carefully, and personally I don't think it's a very wise—"

"Will you look at that? Turning into a pumpkin already."

"You're fracturing your fairy tale. The coach turned back into a pumpkin, not Cinderella."

"What'd she turn into?"

"She didn't turn into anything. She was always the same, but her clothes changed, and her hairstyle."

"So I was close." Tony grinned at her as he climbed the steps. "And I have to get you inside before the spell wears off."

"What spell?"

He set her down and produced a key from his pocket. "My spell, lady." He stuck the key in the lock. "I'm the sexy loser who's going to destroy your good sense with great sex, remember?"

Her knees grew weak. "That was just a figure of speech. This is—"

"This is the best thing for your scheme. You really are a terrible liar, so let me do you a favor and make an honest woman of you."

"Listen, I—"

He kissed her as he opened the door and pushed her through it. When he kicked the door closed and managed to get her onto the bed in two seconds flat, she began to realize that a rational discussion was going to be somewhat of a challenge, especially when Tony's direct course of action felt so good.

There were no lights on in the cottage, but apparently Tony was a man used to working in the dark. He was also a man who knew his way around zippers and snaps, and they gave way with alarming regularity. She would have stopped his skillful maneuvers and initiated a discussion if she could just find a moment to collect her thoughts. With his tongue dipping so provocatively into her mouth, she couldn't seem to think at all.

Even more dismaying, she accidentally started tugging at his clothes, and once she'd started down that road it became a sort of obsession to get to the basics of warm skin and flexing muscle. He seemed perfectly willing to help her in that endeavor. Quicker than a judge could swing a gavel they were both naked and twined together on the four-poster, moaning and panting the way they had that morning in the back seat of the Mustang. Only this bed gave Tony room for his moves.

And the man had moves.

Lynn soon realized that the back-seat encounter had only been a sneak preview with the best parts left out. As much as she loved having him kiss her mouth, having him kiss her breasts was even better. The things he was able to do with his tongue and teeth should have been against the law, because sure as the world, they were addictive. And just when she thought having him stroke her breasts was the ultimate pleasure, he put his hand between her thighs and she was forced to change her mind.

She gasped as he slipped his fingers deep inside her. She'd become a quivering, helpless bundle of needs and he was the only one who could hold her together.

He kept up the deep caress as he nibbled his way back to her mouth. "Wanna talk?" he murmured between kisses.

She tunneled her fingers through his dark hair and struggled for breath. "You're bad, Tony."

"Yes, ma'am."

"Very, very…oooh…"

"That's right, baby."

"I can't…resist you."

His voice was warm with pleasure and humor. "Good."

"Lord knows I've tried." She whimpered as he rubbed his thumb over that most sensitive spot of all.

"I know. Don't be afraid, sweetheart," he whispered. "I won't hurt you."

Maybe he was just saying that, she thought. She didn't care, if he'd just keep touching her like this.

He hovered over her mouth, bestowing tantalizing kisses there before moving slowly down her body. When he reached his final destination, she wondered if a person could die from too much pleasure. He filled her with so much sensual delight that she felt as if she might fly into a million pieces.

At the moment when she teetered precariously on the edge of the precipice, ready to fall, he drew back. In seconds he was there above her, his arms braced on either side of her head, his shadowed eyes gazing down at her.

"Lynn," he said, his voice rich with passion.

She moaned and reached for him.

"Lynn," he murmured more gently as he leaned down to touch his lips to hers. Then, with a firm thrust of his hips, he entered her, and she exploded.

13

After cuddling Lynn until she drifted off to sleep, Tony slipped out of bed and into the bathroom. Closing the door and flipping on the light, he filled the sink with warm water and grabbed his can of shaving cream. He'd probably irritated the hell out of her delicate skin, but if he'd stopped to shave, nothing would have happened between them. He planned on having a lot more happen between them before dawn, and the least he could do was come to her clean-shaven.

He was about three-quarters finished when the door opened. Lynn stood in the doorway, blinking in the bright light and looking adorably tousled. As she gazed at him in the mirror, a soft smile curved her full mouth. But she also showed evidence of every place his beard had rubbed over her skin. He winced.

Laying the razor down, he turned. "I'm sorry."

Her smile faded. "So soon?" There was a catch in her voice as she glanced away. "Forget I said that. I knew this would happen, and it's my own fault. Take the convertible. I'm sure Calvin—"

"Whoa!" He took her by the shoulders. "Permission to question the witness."

She gazed up at him, her expression vulnerable. "Permission granted."

"What the hell are you talking about?"

"You're leaving, going back to Michelle. That's why you're shaving."

"Oh my God." He kissed her, getting shaving cream all over both of them. "No," he murmured, wiping the shaving cream from her cheek as he held her close and gazed at her. "I'm shaving because I want to make love to you all night long, and I feel terrible that I've already done so much damage."

The soft light returned to her eyes. "And that's why you said you were sorry? Because of my whisker burn?"

"That's the only thing I'm sorry for, Counselor."

"Oh." The corners of her mouth tilted up.

"I feel terrible about that, though. Is there anything we can do for it?"

"I have some bath oil that helps, and some lotion I can put on."

"I'll start the bathwater if you'll get the oil," he said, running his hands down her back and over her smooth bottom. "You can soak while I finish shaving." He kneaded her bottom with gentle fingers, and felt his own arousal beginning again. "And as for the lotion, it'll be my pleasure to rub it all over your sweet body."

Her lips parted and her eyes darkened with desire.

His heart thudded with joy. If the look in her eyes was any indication, she was in this as deep as he was. "Bath oil," he reminded her, his voice husky.

"Right." She moved out of his embrace with obvious reluctance.

He started the water in the tub and went back to finish his shave. He damn near cut himself again in his eagerness to be done.

Once she climbed into the fragrant tub of warm water, he walked over and crouched beside her. "Let me wash your back."

She handed him the washcloth with a smile.

He didn't stop with her back. That darned washcloth had a mind of its own, creeping around to her breasts, her thighs and the tender spot behind her knees. She started to laugh

when he announced he'd have to climb in the tub with her
to get the job done right.

Much water ended up on the floor, but by the time he'd
washed her completely, her laughter had turned to moans
of pleasure. He continued the campaign as he dried her
gently with a soft towel. Eventually he gave up the task as
he discovered to his delight that the more he dried her off,
the wetter she became. And he still had the lotion to go.

Carrying her from the bathroom, he laid her on the bed
and switched on the bedside lamp. This time they'd have
light.

She tried to pull him down on top of her.

"You need the lotion," he murmured, unhooking her
arms from around his neck. He was throbbing with need,
but he didn't want her skin to be any more irritated than it
already was.

"I need you."

"Lotion first. Where is it?"

"Bathroom counter." She reached out and boldly
stroked his erection.

He groaned.

"Are you sure you want to bother?" She gave him a
wicked smile.

"Yes." He trundled his desire-racked body into the bathroom and found the lotion bottle. Thank God this was the
second time they'd made love, and he had a little control.
That first time he'd been in ravishing mode and it was a
miracle he'd made it last as long as he had. But he needed
to put that soothing lotion on her irritated skin before they
both got carried away again.

He returned to the bedroom and almost abandoned the
cause. She lay on her side amidst the sheets they'd tangled
so thoroughly the last time, and he'd never seen a more
provocative, come-hither pose. Then he looked into her
eyes, and nearly tossed the lotion bottle over his shoulder
so that he could start right in on the main event.

She spoke in a throaty murmur. "I want you, Tony."

He took a deep breath. "And I'm putting this lotion on first." With an effort, he kept a firm hold on the bottle and walked slowly to the bed. "Lie back."

She did, stretching out and lifting her arms over her head. She let them fall gracefully to the pillow. "How's that?"

"Very effective." He squeezed lotion into a shaking palm. Then he rubbed it between his hands to warm it before he brushed a little over her pink cheeks and chin.

She caught his finger between her teeth.

"Lynn…"

"Mmm?" She drew his finger into her mouth and sucked gently.

"Oh, lady." Maybe he hadn't worked as much of an edge off as he'd thought. He glanced over to make sure there was a condom ready on the nightstand. He might need it quick. Last time he'd just about erupted before he could get one out of his jeans pocket.

"I'm doing this lotion thing," he said, pulling his finger from her mouth. "Stay still."

Of course she didn't. And she needed lotion in all his favorite places, places he'd visited lovingly on the first go-round. As he smoothed lotion over her breasts, she arched into his touch, and her nipples tightened. And he had to taste them. Just a little. But once he started suckling on her nipples, the program was in serious jeopardy.

While he still had one or two brain cells working, he hit upon the plan of doing two things at once. That was how he ended up finding out how the lotion tasted, because while he rubbed lotion on one section of her delicious body, he'd lick another part, but sometimes the whole thing got mixed together. That happened more often after she started writhing around on the bed and telling him to forget the blankety-blank lotion and take her. Finally she threatened to call 911.

"Call 911?" he asked, sliding up beside her and putting the lotion bottle on the bedside table. "Why?"

"*Because* I'm going to have…a heart attack…if you don't make love to me…right *now*."

"It's happened," he murmured. "You've become a wild woman."

"And you've become Lotion Man! Will you stop lubricating the chassis and start driving the car?"

"Yeah," he said with a grin, and reached for the condom.

"Finally! Do you need help with that?"

"I do." He remembered the image he'd had when she took his finger into her mouth. He handed her the condom and lay back on the pillow. "A lot of help."

A flame leaped in her eyes. "Hey, the man admits to some needs."

"A few."

"Well, you've come to the right place."

"Somehow I knew that." His heartbeat quickened in anticipation. Then as she slid down on the bed and her warm fingers encircled him, he wondered if he'd been so bright to suggest this when he was already so worked up. He might need to call 911 himself.

She was getting revenge, he decided some moments later as he twisted against the sheets. She was using her tongue in ways he'd never imagined she knew, and he was close to begging in the same tone of voice she'd used. Very close. In fact, he was beyond close. He begged her to put that condom on him *now*.

She was mercifully fast about it. Then she scooted back up beside him and looked him in the eye. "Well?"

He rolled her to her back and moved between her thighs. His voice was thick with desire, his body desperate for release. Yet he paused. "I really, really want you right now," he said.

"So, go."

"I will, but first…" His heart pounded relentlessly, making it hard to breathe. "I need to know this isn't just about sex."

She stilled beneath him.

"Is it?" he asked, the blood roaring in his ears.

She reached up and cupped his face in her hands. "No," she murmured. "It isn't just about sex."

"We need to have that straight."

"We do. Now please love me, Tony. Love me good and proper."

AT FIRST Lynn thought the ringing phone in the gray light of dawn was her alarm clock, and she slapped at it, trying to find the snooze button. The receiver toppled off and landed on the table, and the ringing stopped, so Lynn went back to sleep.

But there was a pesky voice, a tiny but persistent voice, calling her name, with exclamation marks. It sounded like Calvin.

"Get out of my dream, nerd," she mumbled.

Tony wrapped a sleepy arm around her. "Don't call me that, sweet cheeks."

"Not you. Calvin."

Tony sat up, wide awake. "Where?"

"In my dream." Slowly she became aware that the Calvin voice was coming out of the receiver lying on the bedside table. "Or maybe not." She started to pick it up.

"Allow me," Tony said as he reached across her and grabbed the receiver. "You have reached the love nest of Lynn and Tony," he said into the phone. "We can't come to the phone right now, so at the sound of the tone, get lost." Then he hung up.

The phone began ringing again.

Tony swore and reached for it again. "If that motivational creep thinks—"

"Wait." Lynn caught his wrist. "Maybe something's wrong."

"Okay, I'll ask."

She continued to grip his wrist. "Let me ask."

He gazed at her.

"Please."

He lay back on the pillow and put his hands behind his head. "He'd better have a really good reason for making this call."

Lynn picked up the receiver. "Hello?"

"Lynn! Another two rings and I was coming over there. It's your mother."

Lynn struggled to a sitting position, her heart racing. "What about her?"

Instantly Tony sat up and put his arm around her shoulders.

"It's not life threatening," Calvin said, "but she picked up a bad case of food poisoning at the restaurant last night."

"Oh no!" She glanced at Tony, who was watching her intently. "Where is she?"

"Your dad took her to the hospital in Flagstaff. He asked me to bring you up there."

"Tony and I will drive right up. Which hospital?"

Tony swung out of bed and snapped on a light, then started getting dressed.

"Lynn, I'm afraid she doesn't want Tony there."

"Then he won't go in." She met Tony's hard gaze. "But he can at least drive—"

"She knew you'd say that, and she begged me to ask you to leave Tony out of this. I'll drive you."

Lynn gazed at Tony. To her mother, he was an irresponsible punk who'd gotten her daughter pregnant. She didn't know that he was a wonderful, caring, loving person and a dedicated professional. She didn't know because Lynn hadn't wanted her to. Now Gladys was sick, and she didn't want to have to think about her daughter with such a sleazy guy. Lynn had to honor that.

"Okay," she said. "I'll meet you in the parking lot in five minutes." She hung up the phone. "Mom is in a Flagstaff hospital with food poisoning, and Calvin is driving me up there."

"How bad is she?"

"He said not too bad, but she wants me there, and I want to be there."

"Of course you do. And I'll take you. If she doesn't want to see me, that's fine. I'll stay outside, but I'm not letting Forbes—"

"Please, Tony." She rummaged through her suitcase and found underwear, shorts and a blouse. She dressed as she talked. "It's for the best. We've created an image of you that isn't palatable to my mother. We can't change that at the moment." She finished buttoning her blouse and looked at him. "I need to do it her way until we get everything straightened out."

She wasn't quite sure what she meant by straightening everything out, but she'd worry about that later. She'd worry about her relationship with Tony later. Right now she had to go comfort her mother.

Tony didn't look happy about the situation, but he nodded. "Okay. Call me the minute you have some news."

She walked over and put a hand on his arm. "You're worried about her, aren't you?"

"Yeah." He ran his fingers through his tousled hair. "I didn't think I'd care what your parents think of me, but I do. It bothers me that she doesn't even want me to drive you up there."

She gave him a quick hug. "Just remember that she doesn't know the real you." She slipped her feet into shoes, ran a comb through her hair and picked up her purse. "I'd better go."

"Lynn, I..."

"What?" She paused.

He shook his head. "Never mind. Go see your mom. And...give her my love."

Her throat felt tight. "I will." She hurried out the door into the early-morning chill.

TONY SAT on the bed and stared at the floor. God, he hoped Gladys was okay. She'd hate the indignity of something like food poisoning, but at least it wasn't usually a serious condition. She'd just be uncomfortable for twenty-four hours.

The timing of her illness was rotten, though. Allowing himself to think of his own situation for a minute, he feared that having Lynn take off in a rush was the worst thing that could have happened. She'd left before he could tell her his feelings, before he could move beyond the fantastic sex and into meaningful lovemaking.

What they'd shared was a terrific beginning, but the next step, from great sex to building a relationship, was critical. She was ready to believe that he was only releasing pent-up frustration over Michelle. He needed time to convince her that what they'd shared was far more than that.

He needed time to make sure that it *was* far more than that, from her perspective, as well. After all, he'd just been kicked in the teeth by one woman. He should probably be exercising some caution himself. Yeah, right. It was probably too late for caution. He was quite sure Lynn had loved his technique. But the truth was...he wanted her to love him.

He got up and walked over to the window. The sun was just coming up, reflecting off puddles along the path winding between the cottages. Apparently it had rained during the night. He opened the window and took a sniff of the sweet smell of damp earth and grass. He probably wouldn't have noticed a hurricane, he thought with a grimace. Lynn had absorbed every particle of his attention, and dammit, he wanted her here right now.

But her mother needed her, and he shouldn't think such selfish things. She probably wouldn't be able to call for another hour or so, and it was dumb to stay cooped up in the cottage for that long. He decided to see if he could rustle up a cup of coffee.

As he walked past Gladys and Bud's cottage, he noticed their window was open, too. Bud had probably been too distracted to close it before they left. Tony hoped Gladys's illness would help to bring the couple closer together. He thought they were moving in that direction, and he felt good about that. But he wasn't sure where that left him with Lynn, once the need for their charade was over.

A burst of delighted female laughter filled the morning. Tony smiled, thinking how much it sounded like Gladys. Soon she'd be laughing again, though, and—wait a minute. The sound came again. Dammit, that *was* Gladys.

Her voice floated out the open window. "Boop, boop, b-o-o-p," she said in a low, sexy tone. "You're my little Budikins, aren't you?" Then she laughed again.

"What'dya know?" Bud said, chuckling. "An undiscovered formation."

"Let's call it—"

"Hey!" Tony barreled up to their door, oblivious to what he might be interrupting. He pounded on the door. "Gladys! Bud!"

After lots of scurrying noises, the door opened a crack and a very disheveled Gladys peeked out. "What's wrong?"

"You're okay?" Tony asked.

"I'm terrific, but you don't look so hot. Why're you pounding on our door at this hour?"

Tony swore and glanced toward the parking lot. Of course the Lincoln Town Car was gone. "Calvin's got Lynn." His eyes narrowed. "Or did you know that?"

Gladys pulled her bathrobe closer together and opened the door. "I don't know anything about Calvin and Lynn. Button up, Bud. Something's happened."

"So you don't have food poisoning?"

Gladys looked so totally confused that Tony believed in her innocence.

"Then Calvin made it all up so he could get Lynn alone." Tony felt in his pocket for the keys to the Mustang. "If you'll just point me in the direction of Flagstaff, I'll—"

"Hold it." Gladys finished tying her bathrobe and pulled him inside the room. "Calvin's not a serial killer. Let's take a minute to discuss this."

"How do you know he's not?"

"Oh, for goodness' sake. You're overreacting because you feel possessive about Lynn, which is understandable. But Calvin won't hurt her. He probably wants to take her out for breakfast and discuss her...personal power."

"I'd love to take him out, and breakfast wouldn't be involved." Tony glanced around the cottage and noticed that it looked about the way his and Lynn's did—clothes strewn everywhere, the bed a disaster area. Bud was hastily pulling on a pair of plaid shorts over Big Dog boxer shorts. Then Tony peered more closely at Gladys and noticed that her cheeks and chin were the same shade of pink as Lynn's.

Operation Gigolo was a success.

"Listen," he said. "I know you think Forbes hung the moon, but the fact is, he scared Lynn to death by telling her you were in the hospital with food poisoning. I don't care what his motive is, his method sucks. Frankly, I think calling the authorities and filing a kidnapping charge wouldn't be a bad—"

"Have you been drinking, slick?" Bud asked, peering at him.

"Not a drop. Why?"

"You don't sound like a street punk. You sound like you

did the other night, when you and me got stewed to the gills.''

Tony realized that in his agitation he'd forgotten to behave like the bad boy he was supposed to be. But it didn't really matter anymore, now that Gladys and Bud were obviously back together. "Gladys, Bud, I have something to tell you. I'm not really the sleazy guy Lynn told you I was. I'm actually a lawyer, and I work with Lynn at O'Keefe and Perrin.''

Gladys clucked her tongue and shook her head. "Poor boy. You are upset about this Calvin thing, aren't you?''

"Hell, yes! I don't know where he's taken her, or what he plans to do! And you should have seen her face when she thought you were sick. I could wring his neck for putting her through that. I probably won't, because it's not worth going to jail for assault and battery, but I have legal recourse, and I may just pursue it.''

Gladys tapped her finger against her chin and finally looked at Bud. "What do they call that, when people have more than one personality?''

"Schizophrenia.''

Tony went cold. "Good God. Don't tell me you think Calvin is a schizophrenic?''

"No, dear.'' Gladys walked over and patted him on the cheek. "I think you are.''

14

CALVIN SLIPPED his seminar tape into the player the minute they started up the road that wound through Oak Creek Canyon to Flagstaff.

Lynn reached over and pushed the eject button. "Sorry," she said when he glanced at her in surprise. "I don't feel like being motivated this early in the morning, if you don't mind."

"Certainly, Lynn. It's just a habit I have whenever I drive."

"To listen to tapes?"

"More precisely, to listen to my tapes."

"You listen to yourself while you drive?"

He smiled. "I know it must seem egotistical, Lynn."

"Nah." She tried not to breathe too deeply, because his shaving lotion had a real kick to it. He'd obviously shaved and showered before this trip, and she wondered how he'd worked it in under these emergency circumstances.

"The thing is," he told her, "I pump myself up. Listening to myself, I get inspired. It makes sense, because if I don't inspire myself, how can I expect to inspire others?"

"Indeed." Lynn wondered if he'd been this weird when she'd dated him. If so, it didn't say much for her judgment at seventeen. "Whatever works, I guess. Me, I like coffee."

"Did you want to stop for some?"

"No, of course not. We're not on a pleasure trip. I can get coffee after I've had a chance to see Mom and make sure she's okay."

He fished inside his coat. "Here." He shook a stick of gum out of the pack. "This'll perk you up."

"Uh, thanks, but I'll pass."

"Ah, Lynn, you're determined to reject everything I have to offer, aren't you?" He took a stick of gum from the pack, unwrapped it and popped it in his mouth.

"I beg your pardon?"

He sighed dramatically. "No matter if I suggest chewing gum or a rebirth of your spirit, you're just not interested."

"Hey, if you're going to get your feelings all hurt, I'll take the gum."

"The gum is only a symbol, Lynn. A way of reaching out, of saying that I consider you a valuable human being worthy of receiving what life has to offer."

"Life wants to offer me a stick of gum? Wow."

"Now see that? Sarcasm is like an acid, eating away—"

"Calvin, how did my parents get up to Flagstaff? I just realized they didn't have a car."

"The, uh, resort had a van. They went in that."

"Oh."

"Now, Lynn, deep inside you is a core of pure gold. I'm here to mine that gold, Lynn, to find the nuggets of self-esteem just waiting to be—"

"I thought I was a garden and I had to pluck out my weeds."

"That's Lecture Twenty-four. This is Lecture Twenty-eight, and I think it's far more effective. Picture yourself as a mine shaft. A deep, deep—"

"You know what's bothering me?"

"That's it. Let me probe deep into your being, Lynn. Really deep."

"Actually, this is just a surface question. Why did my parents call you instead of me when Mom got sick? I didn't stop to think about it before, but now I'm curious."

"Because your mother has confidence in me, Lynn. After

attending my seminar, she had a rebirth of self-confidence, as I'm sure you are aware.''

"She started hassling my dad about who would be buried on top in their shared grave, if that's what you mean.''

"That's *exactly* what I mean! She seized her power and knew she would no longer settle for second billing on that tombstone!''

"Let me get this straight." Lynn found her tolerance slipping away. "You support her in that petty argument?''

"Where self-esteem is concerned, nothing is petty, Lynn.''

"And that's another thing! We are the only two people in this car, are we not?''

"Correct.''

"Then I find it ridiculous that you have to repeat my name every two seconds, as if I might become confused and think you were talking to somebody else. Of course, maybe you would be talking to somebody else. Maybe in between listening to yourself on tape, you have conversations with yourself. You're just a complete social unit, aren't you?''

"Now you're getting belligerent, Lynn.''

"Don't call me Lynn, dammit!''

"Your name is the glowing representation of all the wonderful things you can be. The wick of your candle is waiting for the match of confidence to be struck, and you'll blaze forth in all your glory, Ly—''

"I'm warning you, buster.''

"Such a shame. All that promise you had as a young woman, and you're reduced to this belligerent bundle of insecurity.''

Lynn clenched her hands and fought for control of her temper. "Look, I appreciate you giving me a ride to Flagstaff, but I don't appreciate having you use this opportunity to sell me your motivational program. My self-esteem nuggets don't need mining, and the wick of my candle doesn't need lighting, thank you very much. I'd like to consider the subject of my personal growth closed.''

"But I have the answer to your problem!"

"I have no problem except how to survive this ride to Flagstaff without choking you to death, which would seriously interfere with the proper running of this pimp-mobile you rented."

"All right, I'll work with your anger. Anger can stimulate change." He flipped on the turn signal and veered the car onto an unpaved side road.

"Where the hell are you going?"

"The question is, where are you going on the road of life?"

She nearly hit her head on the roof as the car jounced through a puddle of water. "I'd settle for knowing where I'm going on the road to Flagstaff. Is this some shortcut? I really don't believe in shortcuts."

"And you're so right! I was trying to take a shortcut, thinking I could work my program and drive at the same time. Maybe someday I'll have that kind of power, but I haven't perfected the techniques enough yet." The car fishtailed on the muddy road.

She turned toward him. "You pulled off the road so that you could do a better job of mining my nuggets of self-esteem?"

The wheels of the Town Car spun in place, and he switched off the engine to gaze at her. "Yes, I did."

"You egotistical idiot. My mother is lying sick in Flagstaff, and you—" She stopped cold as the truth finally dawned on her. He was too spit-shined to have been called out of bed on an emergency. And her parents would have contacted her, not this maniac, so that she could have driven them in the Mustang. "My mother's not sick, is she?"

He unbuckled his seat belt. "Extreme measures were called for, Lynn."

"Don't you come near me, you creepo. Do my parents know what you're up to?"

"Not exactly, but they've told me how concerned they are, and your mother flew me out here with the understanding that I'd do my utmost."

"So you kidnapped me? Are you insane?"

"I change people's lives, Lynn." He maneuvered across the console. "Let me change yours."

"Ugh." She pushed at him. "That shaving lotion should be regulated by the EPA. I'm not interested, Calvin. Go away."

He reached for her again. "You think you're unworthy of me, because of the baby."

"Oh, yeah, that's it." She shoved him away again. "Buy a clue, would you? I'm not interested in a grope session. At this rate, you're going to swallow your gum, and I know how you hate that."

"I don't mind about the baby." He lunged forward and tried to grab her. By now he was breathing hard. "In fact...thinking about you...being with child...excites me."

She put her hand on his cheek and turned his head away before he could kiss her. "I can see that. Now either you stop assaulting me this minute, or when we dig this car out of the mud and get back to civilization, I'll have you arrested for attempted rape. I don't think that'll do much for your seminar-tape sales, do you?" The guy had the arms of an octopus, she thought, struggling to keep his hands away from her breasts. Another minute and she'd put her knee in his groin, but that was a last resort.

"Oh, Lynn," he moaned, grappling with her again. "Let me touch my match to your wick, let me—*ooof!*" He was suddenly wrenched away and yanked out the door.

Lynn gasped as she realized the yanker was Tony, who had miraculously come to her rescue. Tony's fist connected with Calvin's jaw and Calvin crumpled into the mud.

Tony immediately leaned over Calvin's inert form and ducked inside the car. "You okay, sugarcakes?"

She smiled with relief. She probably could have handled Calvin, but she needed help getting out of the mud. "I'm fine, but what about the old wick-lighter, there?"

"His matches are all wet." He touched her face. "You're sure he didn't hurt you?"

"I'm sure." She caught his hand and kissed his scraped knuckles. "But you'd better check him and make sure you didn't do any permanent damage. That's some right hook you have."

"That's some corny line he's got. Touch his match to your wick? The guy needs a scriptwriter."

"Nice work, slick," Bud said, coming up behind him.

"Thanks, Bud." Tony backed out of the car and shook Bud's hand. "Want to give me a hand? We'll shove him in the back seat."

"I have a better idea. Let's shove him over the nearest lookout point," Bud said.

Lynn unfastened her seat belt and stepped gingerly out onto the muddy road. "Much as I like that suggestion, we'd better not."

"Here I come!" Gladys called as she hobbled through the mud toward the Lincoln. "I know CPR! Is anybody bleeding? I can make a tourniquet with my bra."

"Save your underwear for a better cause, Gladys," Bud said. "Like using it as a tow rope to get us all out of here. I told hotshot, here, not to take this road at sixty miles an hour, but he was driving like A. J. Foyt, and now we're all in up to our hubcaps."

Lynn's heart squeezed as she glanced across the hood of the car at Tony. He'd been driving like a maniac to save her. "I guess you figured things out, huh?"

"Not until I walked past your parents' cottage and heard your mother laugh and call your dad *Budikins*." He gave Lynn a glance filled with meaning.

"Budikins?" Lynn stared at her father, who flushed bright red. Then she looked more closely at her mother and discovered her mother was also blushing, but that didn't account for all the pink on her face. "Oh my God." She laughed with delight and longed to hug Tony, but they were separated by a big car and lots of mud.

"All things considered," Tony said carefully, gazing at her, "I decided I could let them know I'm a lawyer."

She gulped, and the whole scene seemed to freeze in place for a moment as everyone's attention focused on her.

And she had no idea what to say. She'd never deliberately lied to her parents before, and maybe now their trust would be forever shaken. In the original plan, she hadn't intended to tell them. She'd simply meant to explain that she'd broken up with Tony and miscarried the imaginary love child. Now she realized she couldn't do that and leave them with a bad image of Tony, but she'd have preferred a chance to prepare them for the truth.

Tony's expression darkened at her continued silence. Finally he sighed. "But they don't believe me," he said.

"They don't?" She felt giddy with relief. She'd have a chance to gradually work up to an admission of guilt.

"Apparently you told them that I sometimes imagine that I'm a lawyer, and now they think I'm schizophrenic."

"Oh dear."

"And that I sometimes like wearing your underwear. On weekends."

She deeply regretted that little ad-lib. She'd clear it all up at some point, but now didn't seem like the right time. Her parents had just barely reunited, and she didn't want anything to upset that delicate state of affairs. Still, she couldn't let them go on thinking Tony was mentally ill.

She directed her attention to her parents. "Tony's had some training in the law," she said. A quick glance back at Tony told her that he wasn't happy with that response.

He wanted her to make a clean breast of everything, obviously. "And the underwear thing was a joke."

"Yeah, that's me," Tony said. "A real clown."

Her glanced snapped to his. "Tony, I—"

Calvin groaned and Tony broke eye contact with her as he turned to Bud. "Ready?"

"Let's load him."

Lynn hated the way Tony had looked at her, as if she'd completely failed him. Racked with indecision, she watched Tony and her father get Calvin in the back seat of the Lincoln. The two worked well together, and it was the first time she ever remembered her father having genuine respect for one of her boyfriends. How ironic that it was the one she'd set up to be her father's worst nightmare.

But Tony's inherent goodness had shone through the facade, winning over her father in spite of himself. And Tony had won her over, as well. If she let herself, she'd be head over heels in love with him. But she didn't dare allow herself that luxury, not so soon after his divorce from Michelle, a woman he'd loved with all his heart. He might still love her, Lynn thought. He might go straight back to her after this was all over, leaving Lynn with a broken heart. That thought didn't completely excuse her behavior today, but it helped ease the guilt.

Once Calvin was deposited in the back of the Lincoln, the men struggled to free at least one of the cars. They stationed Lynn in the driver's seat of the Lincoln and Gladys in the Mustang, while they tried to rock and push first one then the other out of the muck.

Finally, all four of them stood looking at the mired cars in defeat.

"We're not that far from civilization," Tony said. "I remember passing a bunch of private cabins tucked away in the woods. I'll walk down the road until I find one."

"I'll go with you," Bud said.

"That's okay, Dad." Lynn saw an opportunity to explain

her position to Tony. "You stay here with Mom, and I'll go with Tony."

"I think it would be better if Bud went with me," Tony said.

She felt as if she'd been slapped. He didn't want her to go with him. He was either upset that she hadn't told her parents the truth, or he'd already decided his heart still belonged to Michelle. She'd tried to prepare herself for that second possibility, but apparently she hadn't succeeded. The idea that he might really be in love with Michelle ripped through her like a shotgun blast.

"Okay," she said, not looking at him. "Mom and I will hold down the fort and keep an eye on Calvin."

"Yeah," Gladys said, flexing her fingers. "I wouldn't mind having a reason to hit him, myself."

Bud walked over to Gladys and gave her a kiss right in front of Lynn and Tony. "Go easy on the guy, frizz woman," he murmured.

"You take care of yourself, chrome-dome," Gladys said, pinching his cheek.

Lynn's joy at the obvious love between her parents was tempered by a hollow ache as she realized that Tony made no attempt to bid her goodbye at all. As she and her mother leaned against the trunk of the Mustang and watched the men walk down the road, she fought tears.

"That boy is crazy about you," her mother said.

Lynn's throat was tight. "Oh, I don't know about that."

"I never thought I'd say so, but he might make you a good husband, after all."

"Mmm." Lynn didn't trust herself to answer.

"And they have wonderful doctors for his condition, and new drugs. We'll just keep our fingers crossed that he doesn't pass on the tendency to little Stephanie." Gladys put her arm around Lynn and gave her a hug. "We'll be a wonderful family, all of us. Just wait and see."

Lynn couldn't control the tear that escaped and rolled down her cheek.

"There, there," Gladys said, wiping it away. "It's perfectly natural to be weepy when you're in the family way. Don't be embarrassed, honey."

Giving in to her distress, Lynn turned her face into the familiar comfort of her mother's shoulder and cried.

BUD RETURNED with the tow-truck driver, but Tony didn't. Bud explained with a wink at Lynn that Tony had caught a ride back to the resort so he could "take care of some things." Bud speculated that it would be a champagne breakfast served in the cottage.

Lynn had no such illusions. When she walked into an empty cottage and found Tony's note propped on the nightstand, she wasn't surprised. She picked it up with trembling fingers and stared at the brief message.

Lynn
Mission accomplished. Now we can each get back to our normal lives.

Best,
Tony

He'd even left her a kiss-off gift, the beaded earrings she'd admired on their first night in Sedona. Now he could get back to Michelle with a clear conscience, she thought as a sob filled her throat. And that's when she knew that all her famous self-control had deserted her. She'd tried so hard to keep herself from falling for Tony.

She'd failed.

15

AT THE OFFICE Tony was polite but distant. Sometimes, when Lynn watched him coming down the hall toward her, she'd see a shadow of the sexy bad boy who had made such wonderful love to her that night in Sedona. Then he'd come closer, and his businesslike manner and crisp attire would dispel the illusion.

Lynn told her parents that she and Tony were finished and she'd miscarried. They showered her with sympathy, and she discovered she needed every bit of it. She didn't have to fake a broken heart, after all.

When her parents decided to renew their wedding vows in Sedona a few months later, she knew it would be one of the best and worst experiences of her life. Watching her parents pledge their love would be heaven, while visiting a place that reminded her of Tony's lovemaking would be hell. But of course she had to be there, especially after her mother asked her to be the maid of honor.

She managed to keep her spirits up through the plane ride to Arizona and the drive to Sedona. Her parents had scheduled the ceremony for that very afternoon, to maximize their honeymoon time, as they coyly put it. Lynn wondered if they realized they'd booked her into the same cottage she'd shared with Tony, but she was so busy getting dressed for the ceremony that she didn't have time for bittersweet memories to overwhelm her. She knew they'd hit later, when she was alone, but for now she would concentrate on her parents' happiness.

Finally, dressed in a simple suit in hunter green, she stood inside the resort's creekside gazebo holding a small bouquet of daisies. To her left was the minister, and on the minister's right stood her father, his bald head glistening with nervous perspiration and smiles constantly lighting up his expression. His sport coat was slightly out of fashion and his tie was a little loud, but Lynn thought she'd never seen a more handsome groom.

Outside the gazebo a few guests sat on folding chairs. Bud and Gladys had flown in the members of their bowling team and their closest neighbors for the ceremony. They'd told Lynn they helped finance the whole thing with money from the sale of the single cemetery plot that neither of them wanted anymore.

The taped wedding march sounded through a pair of outdoor speakers, and Lynn's heart surged with joy at the prospect of watching her mother walk out of the lodge and down the red carpet that served as an aisle between the rows of folding chairs. So what if her mother's dress was a startling shade of chartreuse? Then it seemed to Lynn that her heart stopped beating altogether.

Her mother came out on the arm of Tony Russo.

Lynn's bouquet of daisies fell from her nerveless fingers and she grasped the railing of the gazebo for support as her knees buckled.

"Stop the music!" her father shouted, and the wedding march ceased.

He hurried over to her, and soon she was surrounded by everyone, including Tony and her mother.

"Are you okay, Peanut?" her father asked, propping her up against the gazebo railing.

"I...I..." She stared at Tony. "What's he doing here?"

"He was an important reason why we got back together, sweetheart," her mother said, smoothing Lynn's cheek. "So we asked him to be here today. He graciously agreed."

"But we didn't ask that motivational moron," her father

said quickly. "We decided we could do without anybody seizing any power today."

"Oh." Lynn swallowed and took a deep breath. She could get through this, for her parents' sake. "Okay, I understand. I was just…surprised. I'm sorry I screwed up the wedding march. Can we start over?"

"You bet," said the minister. "Back to your places, everyone."

"You'll need this," Tony said, handing her the bouquet. Their fingers touched briefly, and he held her gaze. A lock of his hair fell over his forehead, and she became aware that he was playing the gigolo role once again. He'd bowed to convention by putting on a sport coat, but under it he wore a T-shirt and jeans.

"Don't worry," he murmured. "They still don't know." Then he offered Gladys his arm and they started back up the aisle.

She stood motionless, stunned by his self-sacrifice. Even though she'd let her parents continue to believe he was an aimless punk, a lunatic and a potential transvestite, he'd kept her secret and agreed to come here, as a special favor to her parents…and, apparently, to her. As if the clouds had suddenly cleared from her mind, she knew what she had to do.

"Wait a minute!" she called out. "As long as we've interrupted the ceremony, I'd like to take this moment to make an announcement."

Tony and her mother turned, and all the guests paused in the act of rearranging themselves in the chairs.

"My parents may have told you that the man escorting my mother to the altar is Tony Russo, my ex-fiancé, a man of few prospects but a heart of gold." She looked at Tony, whose eyes widened. "He does have a heart of gold, but he has prospects coming out his ears. He's a valued member of the law firm of O'Keefe and Perrin. He's been a colleague of mine for three years, and when I wanted to stage a little...charade to bring my parents back together, he agreed to play the part of my gigolo boyfriend. He played it so well that when he finally told my mother and father that he was a lawyer, they wouldn't believe him. I was too cowardly to admit I'd lied about the whole thing, and I wouldn't support his claim.''

She took a deep breath. ''I'd like to take this opportunity to thank you, Tony, from the bottom of my heart, for your unselfish behavior. I probably don't deserve your friendship after the way I behaved, but I...would like a second chance to prove I can be a good friend.''

Gradually the surprise in Tony's expression was replaced by warmth and a slow, steady smile. Lynn warned herself not to read anything but friendship into that smile, but her heart beat faster, nevertheless.

Bud and Gladys stared at Tony, and then at Lynn.

''You lied to us, Peanut?'' her father said in amazement. ''You never lie.''

''I did this time.'' She found the courage to look at him. ''And my only defense is that I did it out of love. I thought if I misbehaved, you and Mom would pull together to get me in line, and you'd forget your differences.''

''Oh, honey,'' her mother said, running up into the gazebo again and putting her arms around Lynn. ''Oh, sweetheart, I can't believe that you sacrificed your principles for us.''

''Yes, Gladys,'' Bud said, coming over to stand beside them. ''But she did sacrifice them, didn't she? This is like using a weighted bowling ball! This is like—Gigologate, Gladys! It's huge!''

''Oh, cool your jets, as Tony would say.'' Gladys drew back to smile at her daughter. ''Can't you see how much your little girl loves you?''

''I think she belongs on restriction for this, Gladys.''

In spite of everything, Lynn found herself starting to giggle. "You can't put me on restriction, guys. I'm twenty-nine years old. I'm—"

"Oh yes we can." Gladys exchanged a glance with Bud. "I agree with your father. After this ceremony, you'll go directly to your room and stay there."

"This is outrageous! What if I refuse?"

Gladys gave her a stern look. "You're disrupting our ceremony, Lynn, sweetheart. Now, be quiet and accept your punishment, like a good girl."

"I won't! I—"

"Peanut," her father said. "We know what's best. Now let's just get on with this ceremony so we don't keep everyone waiting, okay?"

She decided her parents were certifiable, but the scene was becoming embarrassing. "Okay. Let's do it."

Gladys patted her arm. "Good girl."

Despite her parents' odd behavior and the unsettling fact that Tony was there, Lynn found herself moved to tears as her parents promised to love and cherish each other. Even her laughter was touched with tears when the minister read the inserted line "in sickness and health, and bad hair days." She glanced at Tony once during the ceremony and discovered he seemed as moved by it as she was. He was probably thinking about Michelle, she concluded.

The recessional played and her parents walked down the aisle as their friends stood and applauded.

Tony offered his arm to Lynn, and she took it, although touching him was such sweet torture that she vowed to turn loose the minute she could gracefully do so. At the end of the red-carpet aisle she started to slip away from him, but he held her fast.

She struggled to free her arm. "Tony, I think it would be best if—"

"Your mother put me in charge of making sure you went straight to your room. You're on restriction, honey bunch."

He started propelling her over the grass and onto the path leading to her cottage.

Lynn glanced back at the crowd of people and noticed both her parents looking at her and smiling. "Oh, for heaven's sake. Let me go, Tony. My parents are insane, as you well know."

"Actually, they're two of the sanest people I've ever met." He continued to half guide, half drag her toward the cottage.

"Look, if I'm supposed to isolate myself in the cottage, I'll do it for a while, just to keep the peace. But you can go back to the group. Besides, I'm sure Michelle wouldn't appreciate you escorting me around, now that you two—"

"I haven't seen Michelle since that night I told you about, before we came to Sedona the first time."

She stopped dead in her tracks, her heart pounding. "Could you repeat that, please?"

He glanced down at her. "I'm not involved with Michelle. I no longer love Michelle. Is that clear enough for you?"

"But—but in your note, you said we could each return to our normal lives."

"Being lawyers, being colleagues. My ego wasn't in very good shape concerning women, and when you didn't tell your parents the truth, I figured you didn't want to continue being lovers."

"But I did!" she blurted out. Then she flushed. "I mean…"

He smiled, and an unmistakable light of love burned in his eyes. "That's what your parents said. They got my home phone number from directory assistance and we've been in touch ever since that weekend. Lynn, they staged this renewal of their vows just to try to get us back together."

"You're kidding."

"No." He faced her and put his hands on her shoulders.

"They seemed to think that our breakup—" his gaze roved her face "—broke your heart."

"Oh, Tony."

He cupped her face in both hands. "I know it broke mine."

Tears of happiness filled her eyes. "I love you so much, Tony. You have to believe me."

"I do." He stroked his thumb gently over her cheek. "I was afraid it was just wishful thinking on your parents' part, until you admitted lying to them, and you did it in front of a bunch of people, too. You must have hated that."

"I did hate it, but not as much as I love you. And if you don't kiss me right this minute I'm going to have to call 911."

"I think this definitely qualifies as an emergency." His lips touched hers with such tenderness that the tears flowed freely down her cheeks. "Don't cry," he murmured, kissing the tears away.

"People always cry at weddings," she said with a sniff.

"How about at proposals?"

"I have a strong feeling they cry at proposals, too."

He reached in his back pocket and pulled out a handkerchief. "Then you'll need this. Please marry me, Lynn. Promise to love and cherish me in sickness and in health and through bad hair days, till death do us part. I love you so much."

In the midst of her sobs of happiness, Lynn managed to say yes.

"Good. Now it's time for you to go on restriction."

She blew her nose. "What did you say?"

He swept her up in his arms and carried her up to the porch of their cottage. "I promised your mother you would stay in your room until tomorrow...with me."

She grew dizzy with excitement. "Punishment is hell, isn't it?"

"And she expects to see a serious case of whisker burn in the morning."

Lynn smiled up at him. "I guess Mom knows best, after all."

Head Down Under for twelve tales of heated romance in beautiful and untamed Australia!

Here's a sneak preview of the first novel in THE AUSTRALIANS

Outback Heat by Emma Darcy
available July 1998

'HAVE I DONE something wrong?' Angie persisted, wishing Taylor would emit a sense of camaraderie instead of holding an impenetrable reserve.

'Not at all,' he assured her. 'I would say a lot of things right. You seem to be fitting into our little Outback community very well. I've heard only good things about you.'

'They're nice people,' she said sincerely. Only the Maguire family kept her shut out of their hearts.

'Yes,' he agreed. 'Though I appreciate it's taken considerable effort from you. It is a world away from what you're used to.'

The control Angie had been exerting over her feelings snapped. He wasn't as blatant as his aunt in his prejudice against her but she'd felt it coming through every word he'd spoken and she didn't deserve any of it.

'Don't judge me by your wife!'

His jaw jerked. A flicker of some dark emotion destroyed the steady power of his probing gaze.

'No two people are the same. If you don't know that, you're a man of very limited vision. So I come from the city as your wife did! That doesn't stop me from being an individual in my own right.'

She straightened up, proudly defiant, furiously angry with the situation. 'I'm *me*. Angie Cordell. And it's time you took the blinkers off your eyes, Taylor Maguire.'

Then she whirled away from him, too agitated by the explosive expulsion of her emotion to keep facing him.

The storm outside hadn't yet eased. There was nowhere to go. She stopped at the window, staring blindly at the torrential rain. The thundering on the roof was almost deafening but it wasn't as loud as the silence behind her.

'You want me to go, don't you? You've given me a month's respite and now you want me to leave and channel my energies somewhere else.'

'I didn't say that, Angie.'

'You were working your way around it.' Bitterness at his tactics spewed the suspicion. 'Do you have your first choice of governess waiting in the wings?'

'No. I said I'd give you a chance.'

'Have you?' She swung around to face him. 'Have you really, Taylor?'

He hadn't moved. He didn't move now except to make a gesture of appeasement. 'Angie, I was merely trying to ascertain how you felt.'

'Then let me tell you your cynicism was shining through every word.'

He frowned, shook his head. 'I didn't mean to hurt you.' The blue eyes fastened on hers with devastating sincerity. 'I truly did not come in here to take you down or suggest you leave.'

Her heart jiggled painfully. He might be speaking the truth but the judgements were still there, the judgements that ruled his attitude towards her, that kept her shut out of his life, denied any real sharing with him, denied his confidence and trust. She didn't know why it meant so much to her but it did. It did. And the need to fight for justice from him was as much a raging torrent inside her as the rain outside.

Take 4 bestselling love stories FREE

a FREE surprise gift!

Special Limited-time Offer

Mail to Harlequin Reader Service®

3010 Walden Avenue
P.O. Box 1867
Buffalo, N.Y. 14240-1867

YES! Please send me 4 free Harlequin Love and Laughter™ novels and my free surprise gift. Then send me 4 brand-new novels every other month, which I will receive months before they appear in bookstores. Bill me at the low price of $2.90 each plus 25¢ delivery per book and applicable sales tax if any*. That's the complete price and a savings of over 10% off the cover prices—quite a bargain! I understand that accepting the books and gift places me under no obligation ever to buy any books. I can always return a shipment and cancel at any time. Even if I never buy another book from Harlequin, the 4 free books and the surprise gift are mine to keep forever.

102 BPA A7EF

Name	(PLEASE PRINT)	
Address	Apt. No.	
City	State	Zip

This offer is limited to one order per household and not valid to present Love and Laughter™ subscribers. *Terms and prices are subject to change without notice. Sales tax applicable in N.Y.

ULL-397

©1996 Harlequin Enterprises Limited

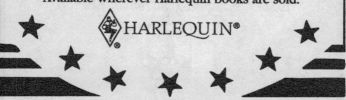

Presents
Extravaganza

25 YEARS!

It's our birthday
and we're celebrating....

Twenty-five years of romance fiction
featuring men of the world and captivating women—
Seduction and passion guaranteed!

Not only are we promising you three months of terrific
books, authors and romance, but as an added **bonus**
with the retail purchase of two Presents® titles,
you can receive a special one-of-a-kind keepsake.
It's our gift to you!

Look in the back pages of any Harlequin Presents® title,
from May to July 1998, for more details.

Available wherever Harlequin books are sold.

◆ HARLEQUIN®

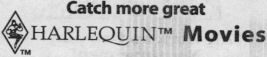

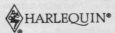

Don't miss these Harlequin favorites by some of our bestselling authors!

LOVE & LAUGH

INTO AUGUST!

#49 REGARDING RITA
Gwen Pemberton
Waitress Rita Lynn is pregnant and her almost-fiancé is out of the country—out of her life, truth be told. Enter widower Nate Morrow, a city-wearied divorce lawyer who thinks he's going to find peace and simplicity in small-town life. Hah! Not in Hooperville, not when every matchmaker in town—which is everyone—thinks he's the answer to the problem "regarding Rita."

#50 GETTIN' LUCKY
Kimberly Raye
Lucky Myers was really *un*lucky in love. So, when she came across a gorgeous cowboy swimming in the buff, she didn't know what to do—run or enjoy the show. And when he asked her to spend time on his ranch, she was floored! That is, until the sexy cowpoke asked her to be his *nanny!*

LOVE & LAUGHTER™